Billionaire's Nanny

Destiny Soul Mates

Summer West

Copyright © 2023 By Summer West

All rights reserved.

No portion of this book may be reproduced, distributed, or transmitted in any form or by any electronic or mechanical means, including information storage and retrieval systems, photocopying, recording, or otherwise without written permission from the author, except for the use of brief quotations in a book review and certain other noncommercial use permitted by copyright law.

This is a work of fiction. Any names, characters, places, or incidents are products of the author's imagination and are used fictiously. Any resemblance to actual persons and things living or dead, present, past or future, locales, or events is entirely coincidental.

<u>Billionaire's Nanny</u>

Cover Designed by: Getcovers

Editors: Jo Gentry, Jeri Phelps

Rv3

PB

Contents

1. Wake-Up Call — 1
2. Music & Messes — 6
3. The Yin to My Yang — 10
4. The Steamy Bean — 16
5. A Sense of Normalcy — 24
6. Key to a New Beginning — 32
7. The Excursions — 36
8. Monday, Monday — 41
9. A Feminine Touch — 46
10. A Symphony of Unplayed Notes — 52
11. The Elephant in the Room — 58
12. The Submission — 62
13. The Green-Eyed Monster — 68
14. The B-Bomb — 74
15. A Surprise from the Past — 81

16.	Impossible to Resist	87
17.	Affirmation	90
18.	Falling into Place	95
19.	Silent Farewell	101
20.	The Last Time	106
21.	An Empty Space	110
22.	Back to the Past	115
23.	A Revelation	121
24.	The End of the Past	127
25.	A Bond Stronger Than Fear	130
26.	The Warmth of Home	135
27.	Bathed in Love	140
28.	Epilogue	147

1

WAKE-UP CALL

ELLA

How has my world come to this? Alone, cold and hungry with nothing but this beat up car to protect me from the freezing winds whirling outside. No money, no food, no bed except for this cramped backseat. What was I thinking?

My only refuge is my car. I'm huddled in the backseat with my too-thin jacket snuggled tightly around me. My sigh fogs the inside of the window for a moment before dissipating.

My ramen noodle dinner leaves a sharp lingering smell. I shiver and kick the empty plastic container against the backseat. My car is my bedroom, kitchen, and prison.

I blink at the faint glow of street lamps filtering through fogged windows, casting long, ghostly shadows that echo my hollowness. I choke down the bitterness with stale water from a bottle I've had since who knows when.

I don't remember the last time I broke down and had a good cry. The kind that exhausts and lightens you. Tonight is a great night for self-pity.

My hair sticks to my tear-soaked cheeks. The cold and the sobs make my body shiver.

F... fuck. I choke out a sob between chattering teeth. I cry salty tears on cold skin. That word feels like a release. *Fuck cold, fuck hunger. And fuck my life, especially.*

After wiping my tears, my eyes sting and my heart races. When I'm living on the edge, breakdowns aren't allowed.

I won't let the ghosts of a home I fled, parents who turned into nightmares, and a savior turned abuser catch up with me now. I'm here voluntarily. I chose this freezing two-door misery over four walls of heated hell.

The cracked screen of my second-hand phone distracts me as I look at a list of random gigs and part-time jobs that offer hope. As I click on each listing and write details on a damp legal pad with my stubby pencil, my stomach tightens.

A job offers hope of normalcy and improvement. Beyond instant noodles and car sleeping. Doesn't this struggle matter? It must lead somewhere warm and safe.

Needing warmth, I tighten the jacket. My despair is echoed by the creaking car. I'll persevere. I'll not give in. Not tonight. No way. Because this mess can only be solved one frostbitten night at a time.

As sleep eludes me, I close my eyes and press my forehead against the icy car window. The thin blanket, the cramped backseat, and ravenous hunger conspire against me.

When it finally comes, sleep is short and filled with restless dreams of warmth and real food. Dreams that make waking up to my grim reality even more shocking.

I open my eyes and sit up, my heart pounding loudly. I see the time on my phone. Fuck, fuck! Battery life nonexistent, my phone, my only lifeline, my alarm clock, has died overnight.

One interview, one chance to escape this miserable life, and I may be late. I rush to gather myself. I put away the empty noodle container, find a hair tie, and find my resume, which holds my only hope.

I climb into the front seat and turn the key, silently praying to anyone listening. The old car grumbles, refusing to start. I try again, but the engine dies. I stubbornly swallow panic. *Not today, car, not today.*

I turn the key again, my heart pounding in time with the engine. Each failure stings. The fifth keyturn works. The engine rumbles like a grizzled beast waking up. I breathe a shaky sigh and pat the dashboard, thanking my stubborn pet.

Tall streetlights illuminate the roads in early morning darkness. The world is holding its breath before the day begins. No time to appreciate it. Every second counts toward missed opportunity.

I traverse the empty streets, rehearsing interview questions that make me more anxious. I grip the steering wheel until my fingers are white as my chest tightens. My stomach churns at the thought of screwing up and losing this chance because of my nervous jitters.

The car's weak heater fights the early morning chill, warming my layers. As the nerves fade, my fingers relax on the steering wheel. Maybe it's knowing I've done this before. It's a job interview.

My rearview mirror confirms the worst as I pull up outside the building. I have dark circles under my eyes and wild hair from sleepless nights and endless worries. But my determination is new.

I take one last breath and step out of my car-turned-home, clutching my shoulder bag with my resume protruding like a lifeline. I'm here regardless. Despite cold, hunger, despair.

It's a brief interview, but it's huge for me—a glimmer of hope in a dark life. I must never lose hope.

A small cafe is hiring for serving tables, wiping counters, and taking orders. It's honest and pays. That's the most important thing.

The café welcomes me with warmth and the smell of fresh coffee, but the knot in my stomach remains. Behind the counter, a stern blonde woman in a crisp shirt and skirt purses her lips.

She inspects me with a sneer. "Who are you?" she asks condescendingly.

"I'm Ella... Ella Parker," I say.

"Oh, you're late," she snaps, checking her wristwatch. "No interview."

I'm stunned. "What? I'm only four minutes late!" I object, checking my worn-out watch, which reads 6:04.

She crinkles her nose and waves me away. "Sweetie, you didn't shower or comb your hair. No job, but I'll give you a cup of coffee for the road. Bright eyes, not sad sacks, for the morning shift."

I'm blushing. "I'm sorry. Please give me another chance," my voice cracking. "I'm desperate. I really need this job. I can't lose this chance."

She scoffs, "Ellie?"

"Ella," I correct her, growing impatient.

"Whatever. This is not the Second-Chance Cafe. I'm sorry."

One heartbeat turns anxiety into anger. I ignore the voice inside telling me to leave quietly, hide my feelings, hold my tears, and be silent.

"You know what? Fuck you and your stupid-ass job," I shout. "I don't fucking need a job working for a hard-ass Miss Perfect Pants anyway! And I'd rather drink rainwater than coffee from your fucking hands."

The woman's shocked and outraged face would have been hilarious under different circumstances. As I turn away and leave, I see the cook smiling through the service window and a waitress giving me a discreet thumbs up.

I bolt from the cafe, my heart pounding like a metronome. Air, please. My little spectacle's adrenaline is fading, leaving me hollow and exposed. Winter air bites my cheeks, but it's better than the stale, grease-scented heat inside.

A woman's voice breaks my mental trance. "Are you okay, honey?" I turn to see a coatless woman with worry-lined bright eyes. She has a dark brown ponytail and looks to be my age or slightly older. She's a cafe customer.

I nod, barely smiling. "I'm fine. Thank you."

She moves closer, her hands awkwardly hanging by her side as if she's unsure if she should reach out. "I'm Alice," she says. Her demeanor calms my racing heart.

"I'm Ella," I say, wondering how this stranger can help my mess.

"I saw Madge reject you in the cafe. If it helps, she's a bear. You're probably better off without a job in this place." Alice points to my backpack's faded Lennox College tag. "Are you a student?"

"Yes, part-time grad student," I reply, curious.

"Oh, what a coincidence!" she exclaims with recognition. "My big brother teaches there. His name is Ethan. Ethan Hartley. Heard of him?"

I scoff. I haven't.

She smiles knowingly. "How about I contact him? He might be able to help you get a job on campus. They always need help somewhere. Perhaps the cafeteria or library?"

My chest burns with unexpected hope. "Would you really help me?" I'm astonished.

"Of course," Alice smiles. She pulls a business card from her bag. "My card. Call me after 8 a.m. We can talk. I'll get your info and give it to my brother, okay?"

"Thanks, Alice." I take the card, touching her beautifully manicured hand. *The Zen Yoga Tree* is elegantly scripted in gold on the pale lavender card.

I'm amazed at Alice's unexpected lifeline as she walks away. A cautious hope and comfort replace adrenaline.

I'm alone again, clutching the business card like it's my last hope. Today, as I look at the card under a street lamp, I think I might be okay.

I take Alice's business card back to my car and think of her brother. College instructor. Will he help? Will he care? Only a call later today will reveal the answer. Just breathing helps me regroup. The car starts right away this time, and I smile as I drive to the YMCA.

2

MUSIC & MESSES

ETHAN

I wake up to sunlight streaming through the window of my spacious bedroom. I cherish a rare moment of quietude. The calm before the storm. Oliver usually rises early, but today may be an exception. I check the clock: 6:47 a.m., a bit late for him but too early for me.

Suddenly, Oliver's cry pierces the silence, a reluctant start to the day. I groan, dragging myself out of bed. Despite my body's protests, I know Oliver needs me.

As I step toward his room, I pause to admire the view from my window – my grand estate, the sprawling gardens, the beautiful architecture. It nearly takes my breath away every time.

I slip across the hall into Oliver's room. He's curled up in his red racecar bed, a cocoon of blankets and teddy bears. "Morning, Ollie," I whisper, sitting beside him.

His whimpering subsides as he rubs his eyes and looks at me. His blond curls stick up in every direction, and I can't resist smoothing them down.

"Up, Daddy," he mumbles, reaching his arms out for me. I laugh, scooping him into my arms. He's growing fast, but I still cherish these moments. His head rests on my shoulder, and I savor the scent of baby shampoo lingering in his hair.

"Okay, buddy," I say, "let's get breakfast."

We head to the kitchen, greeted by the soft morning light. Dirty dishes from last night and toys scattered all around, but I ignore the mess. Breakfast comes first.

It's not like I can't afford help, but Oliver doesn't take to the people I've interviewed. He clings to me and hides behind me, not even willing to say 'Hi.' So, I handle the mess myself.

I put Oliver in his booster seat, surrounded by colorful toys on the dinette table. His enthusiasm is infectious. I glance at Oliver occasionally as I prepare the scrambled eggs. The kitchen fills with the aroma of eggs and toast.

Once the eggs are cooked to perfection, I give them to Oliver. He's ecstatic, and I can't help but laugh. The morning flows with Oliver's messy eating and non-stop giggles. It's a peaceful day, just the two of us in our little world.

My phone buzzes, and Alice's name pops up. My sister, always a character.

"Morning, Sunshine," I say sarcastically as I clean up the mess Oliver made.

"Cut the crap Ethan, it's almost noon," she retorts, her tone light.

"It's 8:30," I reply, chuckling, as I see Oliver using his scrambled eggs as hair gel.

"Single dad life," she teases, "I miss you both. Yoga is not as fun without my favorite nephew."

"Funny sis...he's your only nephew."

Then her tone turns serious, "Ethan, there's something I need to talk about."

My attention sharpens. "Sure, what's up?" I pause the wiping up of eggs.

"Do you know a student named Ella Parker?" Alice asks cautiously.

" I don't think so, should I?"

"Well, she needs a job. I thought maybe you could help her out at the university?" Alice asks.

"Why?" I raise an eyebrow. "Who is she?"

"She's a friend in need, Ethan. Will you help her?"

I feel guilty for doubting Alice's intentions. "Fine, I'll see what I can do. Give me her contact."

"Thanks, Ethan. You're a good brother."

"Yeah, yeah," I reply, secretly pleased at her approval.

With a promise to call back later, I end the call. Back to the mess. My work-from-home day just got more interesting.

Now with a full stomach, Oliver seems a bit sleepy, so we move into the living room, my make-shift music room. With Oliver on the couch, he's content watching TV so I can work.

I turn on my state-of-the-art mini recording studio, adjust the controls and tune my guitar.

My music students need their weekly assignment today, a piece to learn and prepare for presentation at our next class. As I record the music, I glance at Oliver. He's fallen asleep...peaceful.

Music fills the room, as I edit and upload the file for my students. Music has always been my passion, my refuge, my escape. And now it's my career too.

Oliver has slid into an awkward position, so I go to him and adjust his neck. He still snoozes soundly. I kiss his forehead and retreat to my desk.

My phone chimes, alerting me to Alice's text. Her antics always amuse me.

Ella Parker: 326-627-7613
Good luck, big brother!

Replying quickly, I set my phone aside, Oliver still resting quietly. I move to the couch and drape one arm around Oliver's little body. My phone buzzes again, Alice's reply. But I'm in no rush. For now, I just savor this quiet moment with my son and my music.

3

THE YIN TO MY YANG

ELLA

After parking my car in the farthest spot, I head across the parking lot and wait by the glass door for my friend Stacey. She's busy folding towels at the counter and takes a moment to notice me. She buzzes me in, and I walk up to the counter.

"So, how did the interview go?" she asks.

I just shake my head, roll my eyes, and take the towels she shoves my way.

"Next time," she says, trying to cheer me up putting a bag from Gas-n-Go on top of the towels.

I mouth a "thank you" as I rush to the lockers. I open locker number 44 with my key and grab the plastic bag with my clean clothes before heading to the showers.

After a refreshing shower, I allow myself to indulge in the blueberry muffin from Stacey. I don't know what I would do without Stace.

She works part-time at the Y and sneaks me in to use the showers in the morning, as long as I'm out by 8:00 when the manager arrives. She also lets me keep a locker for my clean clothes and even helps me with laundry in her dorm basement.

We share food, and in return, I use my English talent to help her math brain with English Lit assignments.

I pack up my stuff and wave to Stacey as I leave the Y.

"Library at 10:00!" she calls after me. I nod, swinging my backpack over my shoulder.

ELLA

Stacey and I are sitting at a table in our study spot, surrounded by textbooks and notebooks. My auburn-haired friend is busy with accounting while I struggle through my poetry assignment.

John Donne's "The Flea." I groan and roll my eyes. "Can you believe I'm actually studying this?"

Stacey looks up from her book, her bright green eyes gleaming. "Oh, come on, Ella. It's not that bad. At least it's not Shakespeare."

I scoff. "You're right, it's not Shakespeare. I actually *like* Shakespeare. This is worse. Donne is turning a flea into a confusing metaphor."

Stacey smirks. "I found it kind of... romantic."

"Romantic?" I laugh, finding her perspective amusing. "It's about a flea, Stace."

She picks up the poem and reads with an exaggerated dramatic flair, "Mark but this flea, and mark in this, How little that which thou deny'st me is; It sucked me first, and now sucks thee..."

I can't help but laugh. "Okay, okay, I get it. But seriously, if a guy ever tried to impress me with a flea metaphor, I'd... I'd..." I'm laughing too hard to finish the sentence.

Stacey joins in, our laughter echoing through the library. "Well, at least you're having fun with it," she giggles.

Our laughter fades, and Stacey goes back to her work while I return to the poem. It's still confusing, but now I find it a bit amusing.

The thought of some lovesick poet using a flea to woo his beloved...well, sharing this moment with Stacey makes it less overwhelming. This is the only class Stacey and I share, so it's nice to ponder it together.

Suddenly, the atmosphere changes. Stacey gasps, and I follow her gaze to see Jason Miller, the epitome of a jock, swaggering in.

Stacey sighs dreamily. "Isn't he just divine?"

I raise an eyebrow at her. "Divine? Seriously? You need a thesaurus."

She grins. "Okay, fine, he's hot. Happy?"

I chuckle. "You and your crushes."

Stacey nudges me playfully. "Come on, you've never looked twice at a jock?"

I shrug. "Not really. I've got bigger things on my mind." If Stacey only knew what I've been through with Matt. I've shared the basics with her, but not the horrific details.

She gives me a skeptical look. "Like what?"

"Like finding a job," I reply. "I hope that yoga lady, Alice, helps me out. She sounded nice and sincere this morning."

Stacey laughs, a light, airy sound. "You mean you're actually banking on that? I still believe she's a human trafficker or something. Who just randomly offers to help like that?"

"Cynic! Really, if I can get a job on campus, it would be a lifeline."

We sit in silence, each deep in thought. Stacey's attention is back on Jason, while I find myself rereading Donne's poem. Although our concerns are different, I'm grateful for Stacey's company and her ability to lighten the mood with her humor. Like making human trafficking jokes.

My phone's soft chime breaks the silence. Stacey's head snaps to look at me expectantly.

"Is it the yoga lady?" she asks with a teasing grin.

I unlock my phone and read the message. "It's an unknown number."

Stacey smirks. "Maybe it's your secret admirer."

I roll my eyes and read the message aloud:

> Hello, Ella. This is
> Professor Ethan Hartley.

"Have you heard of him, Stace?"

She shakes her head. "I don't think so. And I know all the professors in our department. He must be in a different department...or a human trafficker," she taunts.

We both burst into laughter, making the situation a little less daunting. Our laughter continues unabated until a stern voice echoes through the quietude of the library. "Shush, ladies! This is a library, not a coffee shop!"

Stace and I look at each other, both biting our lips to keep from laughing harder and being evicted from the library.

My phone buzzes again. Stacey's eyes widen with excitement.

Chastised, we quiet down and reduce our giggles to whispers. Then my phone buzzes again, breaking the silence of the library.

> My sister Alice gave me your
> number. She told me you need
> a job in the college. Are you free to
> talk about this in the afternoon?

Stacey smirks. "Well, of course, you're free. Or you could just tell him you're too engrossed with *The Flea*."

I nod and type my reply.

> Yes, I'm free this afternoon.
> Where should we meet?

His response comes quickly.

> How about
> The Steamy Bean at 2:00?
> We can chat over coffee.

Stacey gives me an amused look. "The professor wants to meet you for coffee?"

"Yes!" I whisper, barely able to contain my excitement. Stacey gives me a high-five of approval.

> That will work for me.
> I look forward to meeting with you.

As we pack up and leave the library, Stacey nudges me playfully. "So, ready to fuel up before your 'hot date' with Professor Hartley?"

I laugh. "Cool it Stace. I'm meeting him so I can afford lunch, remember?"

Stacey's laughter rings out, blending with the distant chatter of other students and the rustle of leaves in the breeze. "Okay, okay, I'll stop. But on one condition, I buy you lunch today. No arguments."

"Fine. As long as it's not ramen noodles. I swear, if I eat one more noodle, I may turn into one."

We head to the campus café, and I can't help but feel a mix of nervousness and excitement. Stacey's company helps me forget about my worries for a while.

As we enter, we're met by the familiar aroma of coffee and fresh-baked pastries. Students and professors alike are gathered around small tables. The whole place buzzes with a comforting energy that makes me feel a little less out of place.

I watch as Stacey excitedly surveys the lunch options on display. She's clad in her favorite oversized sweater that's seen better days, a pair of well-loved jeans, and her hair neatly plaited down one side.

I am in a comfortable pair of high-waisted jeans and a lavender blouse. My hair, a thick curtain of brown, is tied up into a loose bun.

We order lunch and find a corner table to enjoy our lunch – a couple of hearty sandwiches accompanied by a side of fresh salad. It's a simple meal, yet it feels like a feast after my recent diet of canned soup and instant noodles.

Despite my upcoming meeting with Professor Hartley, I feel lighter with Stacey by my side. She has an uncanny ability to make me feel better. She's the yin to my yang, the person who knows when to offer a comforting hug or a well-timed joke.

As we finish our lunch, I'm grateful for this friendship that makes life's challenges a bit easier to bear. With Stacey, I know I'm not alone, no matter how tough things get.

4

THE STEAMY BEAN

ETHAN

Grading papers and answering student emails keeps me busy this afternoon. Preparing for my Ella Parker meeting is just one more thing added to the list. However, seeing "Preschool" on my phone gives me pause.

My home office appears on the screen when I receive the call. Oliver's teacher Miss Jennifer smiles on screen. She possesses saintly patience and angelic kindness. A few stray blonde strands of hair frame her fresh face in a loose ponytail.

"Hello, Mr. Hartley," she says, her voice pleasant but laced with concern that puts me on edge.

"Hi, Miss Jennifer," I say, attempting a grin. "Is everything okay?"

She pauses, and my heart races. "It's Oliver…" she says sympathetically. "He's having a bit of a tough time this afternoon. He's crying and asked if he could speak to you."

My gut tightens with worry and remorse. My son hurts. I almost brought Ollie home from preschool because he was unusually quiet. But I needed work time and I know he needs to socialize with other preschoolers.

Nodding to Miss Jennifer, I swallow my lump. "Of course. Can I talk to him?"

A little, tear-streaked visage replaces her on screen. His beautiful, red-rimmed eyes, a shade of hazel like his mother's, are swollen from sobbing. I'm heartbroken. His chubby fists hold the phone as his lower lip trembles.

"Hey, buddy," I attempt to sound calm. "What's wrong?"

His tearful eyes find mine, and he sobs, "I...I want mama."

My universe shrinks. His comments rekindle my heartache. A lingering, terrible loss.

Blinking, my eyes burn with tears. "I know, Ollie," I choke out. "I know, sweetheart. Mama... Mama can't be here, baby. But you have me. You have Daddy."

Leaning into the phone, he nods. I want to reach through the screen to hold him. But words will have to suffice.

"Look, Champ," I whisper. "I promise you, everything is going to be okay. I'll pick you up real soon. You just need to be a brave boy for a little bit longer."

Hiccups and nods replace his tears. "Okay, daddy."

"And Ollie," I add, "Remember what we always say? 'Always in our hearts', right?"

His little voice repeats, "Always in our hearts."

I inhale and close my eyes. Her loss is still fresh and terrible. It's scabbed over, yet it still hurts like we lost her yesterday.

Lily, my wife, was powerful. Rich, smart, and beautiful. We met while I was a poor musician performing local pubs and she was a young hippy heiress with an artistic heart.

We fell in love instantly, and I was sucked into her world of wealth and riches. With Lily, I could fit into a world I never thought I'd be in.

She was diagnosed with cancer five years after we met. It was an unexpected tragedy. We fought hard and attempted every treatment, but it was not enough. She died six months later.

She died gently in her sleep, with me by her side. Ollie was not even two. We talk about her and look at her picture, so Ollie can remember. It was important to Lily that I not let Ollie forget who she was.

I inherited her fortune, but it never felt right. I never wanted to be defined by material wealth. I kept playing music and returned to the university to teach music.

I try to stay busy every day. She died almost two years ago, and I try to honor her memory every day, in small ways, through Ollie and my music.

I hang up the phone after letting the emotional surge subside. I find my power in the deafening silence. I can't let my son down. Not now, not ever.

My appointment with Ella Parker is a fixed point in my agenda that I had to squeeze into an already busy day. I didn't realize how busy until I was racing to get there. I have only 15 minutes to travel to campus, according to my watch. I brush my hair and put on my jacket, not bothering to check the mirror.

I take the less busy side streets and park two blocks from the college coffee shop. I take in a deep breath of cool, fresh air. After I regain my composure, I practically sprint to my destination.

The Steamy Bean, a popular cafe between the bookstore and the student union, is on the far edge of campus. Its name in green and white curly letters is a welcoming sight.

The bell dings as I open the door and feel the warmth from inside. I take in the smell of freshly ground coffee beans, indie music, and the odd hiss of the espresso machine. Creating a calming atmosphere, it's a relaxing symphony that connects with my senses.

The continuous chatter, laughter and clanging of dishes makes the day seem normal. I search the room for Ella Parker to start the next chapter of my day. Alice hadn't mentioned Ella's appearance, so I quickly pull out my phone and text her.

> Hi Ella. I'm here.
> You here yet?

A response arrives before I have a chance to think too long.

> I'm in the farthest corner
> wearing a lavender blouse.

I put my phone in my pocket and look around the shop. I see a young woman in a lavender blouse sitting under a draped string of fairy lights.

She's drinking coffee and reading a worn copy of The Complete Works of John Donne. Her brown hair is fashioned in a loose bun. Her clear green eyes, enlarged by her glasses, pop up at me as I approach. Her posture straightens as she sets her coffee down.

"Hi, Ella?" I say, smiling as I extend my hand. She hesitates but takes my hand, gripping it warmly.

"Yes, that's me. Professor Hartley, I presume?" Her voice is bright yet nervous.

"Yes, but please, call me Ethan." I sit across from her and put my jacket on the back of the chair. "So, Alice tells me you're looking for a job."

Her shoulders relax when Alice is mentioned. "Yes, I am. I was actually applying for a job at a coffee shop, but..." She hesitates, her cheeks blushing remembering her rude exit. "I was four minutes late and told to forget it."

"And that's when Alice saw you?" I softly prod, noticing her downward stare.

""Yes," she says. "I was quite furious, so I stepped outside to gather myself. Alice came out to talk with me. She suggested a university position might be open, and here we are."

As we talk, I'm intrigued by this young woman Alice has brought into my life. I wonder how much of an impact she'll have on my busy, messy life. She's honest and genuine, which I like.

"Well... As far as I know," I say with disappointment, "all university positions are usually filled before the semester begins. I doubt we can find one for you."

My comments make her face collapse, her eyes downcast and her hands clench in her lap. It's as if I've wounded her, visibly draining her hope and leaving her vulnerable.

I find myself grappling with a surge of sympathy for her. She's a grad student in her early twenties, trying to find a place in this complicated world. And here I am, delivering another blow.

"Do you really...need a job? I mean..." The words spurt out before I can stop myself, the sheer misery in her silence pulling at me. She doesn't answer, but bites her lower lip, her head dropped. "I mean...where do you stay?"

She flinches, barely noticeable, and her eyes, when she finally glances up, show a trace of dread. It's as if I've asked something extremely personal, something she isn't ready to discuss. But my instincts as a father and teacher urge me on.

"You live in a campus dorm, right? Or with your parents?" The instant the question leaves my mouth, I know I've stepped on a landmine. Her eyes fill with tears, her hands quivering as she attempts to maintain her composure.

"I'm sorry... Professor Hartley," she whispers, shaking. "Please excuse me for a moment." She immediately stands up, leaving me at the table with her belongings, and rushes to the restroom.

I feel a strange mix of emotion as she disappears around the corner. I have a surge of empathy for this young woman, a stranger an hour ago, who is fighting unseen demons.

And guilt for pushing her to share more than she's willing. I sit back to ponder. Long afternoon.

She returns after a few minutes, her eyes inflamed, and her composure regained. I sense a new determination. "I don't need your sympathy, Professor Hartley, nor do I need any handouts." Her voice is solid and stronger than before. "But I'm going to level with you because, well, I need to."

She looks out the window at a small, old car parked under a tree. "You see that compact car out there? That's...that's my home. I've been living in it since...well, since my world fell apart."

I choke. Her predicament slams me. Her speech and eyes suddenly make sense. She continues as I sit speechless.

"My parents... they decided that my choices were unacceptable. I don't believe in God and well... they are extremely religious." Her bitterness overpowers her fear.

"They gave me an ultimatum – either repent for my sins or leave the house. My sins are wearing jeans, reading literature, and drinking caffeine. So, I left."

It's everything I can do to stay seated and not reach out to her as I hear her suffering and see her striving to keep strong.

"I am not looking for charity, Professor Hartley," she says, breaking the silence. "To endure and study. To prove to myself that my choices, however painful, have not derailed my goals."

As I listen to Ella's confession, I feel anger at the people who brought her to this point. A part of society with narrow social views. And I feel empathy for this young woman who has shown tremendous courage in the face of adversity.

I realize I can't just sit back and do nothing. I have to do something—not out of pity, but out of respect for her resilience. If I don't, I'll never forgive myself.

Then an idea hits me. The answer is simple, yet it will solve many problems at once. I look at Ella, a glimmer of hope sparkling in my eyes.

"Ella, how would you feel about becoming a nanny? For my 3-year-old son, Oliver," I ask, my heart pounding with anticipation.

She blinks, her brows furrowing. "What? Professor Hartley, you hardly know me." I can see the spark of excitement in her eyes, a possible lifeline.

"True," I concede, wringing my hands. "I've spoken to you enough to see your sincerity and feel your struggles. You need a job, and I need a nanny. I have a large home, so we have plenty of room. Plus, my sister Alice...She thinks highly of you."

"But... I don't have any experience," she stammers. "And your sister only met me today."

"You won't need experience," I promise her, smiling. "Oliver... he's a sweet child. He needs love more than anything else. And I can see in your eyes, Ella, you've got a lot of that to give. Besides, my sister Alice can tell a person's character right away and is rarely wrong about people."

"Alright...Professor Hartley, I... accept."

Relief and uncertainty flood over me, and I smile warmly. "Thank you, Ella. No regrets. You'll be well-paid and live comfortably. I'll provide a room and food and respect your privacy.

"I simply ask that you love and care for Oliver with all the love and compassion you have. Treat him like family, and Ollie and I will welcome you with open arms.

"Oliver's mother died almost two years ago. He hasn't had much of a maternal influence since then. Alice does her best, but she's very busy with The Yoga Tree."

Ella's eyes soften with thanks and empathy. "I'll do my best, Professor Hartley. I won't disappoint you or your son."

"I have no doubt you will do a great job, Ella," I say, patting her shoulder.

With a renewed feeling of purpose, Ella and I discuss the logistics of the transition. The specifics of her moving in with Oliver and me, her schedule, and her compensation.

As we continue, I understand that this is more than an employer-employee relationship. It is a co-op between two people who have faced suffering and are seeking solace and redemption.

I will give Ella the chance she deserves and help her regain her footing.

"That's great, Ella. I'll text you the address. Can you come tonight at 7? Or is that too soon?"

"Yes, I can make it."

"That's good. It's Friday, so we'll have the weekend to get acquainted before the weekday chaos begins."

As I leave the coffee shop, I sense a strange feeling of satisfaction. Maybe I can give Ella a fresh start and Oliver the love and care he deserves. Only time will tell.

5

A Sense of Normalcy

ELLA

6:23 PM. I watch the dashboard clock flash in my cramped worn-out car. My fogged windows reflect the orange sunset outside as the day fades into twilight. An involuntary shiver ripples through me, part temperature drop and part nervousness.

A gentle chime distracts me. I grab my phone from the passenger seat, heart racing. Professor Hartley—Ethan, as he insists—sent me a text. His nicely typed address appears on the screen.

I hesitate before entering the address into my map app. The map voice says, "Fourteen minutes away." One side of me wants to start the car and go, but the fearful, doubting side refuses. I'm too early. Maybe I need time to think.

I pull up Stacey's number. My car's stillness echoes the computerized dialing tones when I push the call button. Stacey answers on the second ring with excitement. "Ella! What's up?

"Hey Stace. Whatcha doing?"

"You sound...different," she says, playful yet concerned.

I inhale to calm my heart. "Professor Hartley...he...offered me a job, Stace. His son's nanny."

There's a pause on the other end. Stacey's high-pitched voice returns. "What?! Are you sure he's not a human trafficker? Ella, did he give you an address? Send it to me now! If you don't call me every hour, I'm calling the cops!"

Despite my anxiety, I laugh at Stacey's usual drama. "Stacey, relax. He's sincere. Ollie is his three-year-old son. He just needs a nanny and a housekeeper. I think...it'll be okay."

We converse more, alleviating the tension in my chest. Stacey's disbelief evolves into acceptance as I explain everything. She has experience babysitting her cousins. So she pledges to answer my nanny questions.

"And Ella, don't forget the assignment," she says as we hang up. "The flea won't analyze itself!" I laugh, promising to complete our English Lit project.

I stare at the car's windshield after the call. The world outside is softly lit. It's time. I turn the key and the engine sputters to life.

I'm ready for anything with a chance for a new career and a better life.

When I arrive at the address, I turn into the driveway. *HOLY SHIT! I can't believe the size of the house. He said he "inherited" it from his wife, but he totally under-played it!*

There's a long curving driveway centered between two lion gargoyles. The drive leads up to the spectacular mansion, the lawn perfectly manicured and landscaped. The house is a very subdued tone of beige stucco, giving it a very sophisticated ambience.

I'm embarrassed driving up this hill toward the stunning house in this junker car. I'm sure Ethan won't want it sitting here at the front entrance for very long. I hope there is a back entrance I can use, so I don't humiliate him with this unsightly car.

I grab my small duffel bag and backpack and take one last look at my car. My heart races as the building's brown exterior looms large in the fading daylight.

It's a sprawling estate, huge for a college professor's house. A sprawling garden is blooming with late-fall colors in front. The house is a picture-perfect image of wealth that both astonishes and intimidates me.

I grip my bags tighter, knocking quietly on the large oak door. Ethan smiles when the door opens. His navy sweater is a sharp contrast to his crisp white shirt underneath. His stubble and dark hair accentuate his powerful jawline. He's handsome, but not a "jock-stud" like Jason Miller in the library today.

A soft giggle sound is behind him. A little figure in Spider-man pajamas appears behind Ethan's leg. Oliver. He has blond hair, but curly hair like his father's and curious hazel eyes.

"Hello, Oliver," I bend down to his level. "I'm Ella. Your new friend." He releases Ethan's leg and smiles shyly.

"El-la," he says slowly. My heart clenches for the first time when he says my name. "I'm Ollie."

"Come in Ella. Welcome to our home."

"Thank you, Professor Hartley...uh...I mean Ethan. This is a beautiful home. Much bigger than I imagined. Should I move my car? It looks quite out of place, being a junker and all."

Ethan chuckles. "Not that it matters, but if you'll pull around back, Ollie and I will meet you in the garage and I will show you where you can park."

Agreeing, I return to my car and wonder what the back of the house will look like. As I follow the drive around to the back, I am even more amazed. What looks like acres of green pasture with a couple of chestnut horses.

I am not much into equine, but these specimens look so beautiful. So peaceful. There is a large pool with a sundeck nearer to the house. Even though the pool is covered for winter, it looks like a fabulous spot to relax in the warmth of summer. *I wonder if I will still be here when the weather turns warm.*

There are 3 extra-wide garage doors at the back of the house. Fortunately, one of them is opening. Ollie runs to the open space and waves his arms overhead. He signals me to follow him to my parking spot.

Sitting in my rust-bucket clunker, I see at least three luxury sedans. *I wonder what is in the other two garages.* Then I see. It's one huge garage with two or three vehicles in each section. SUVs, pickup trucks and one elongated that I assume must be a limousine.

Ethan meets me as I exit and asks if he can help carry my things. *If only I had any **things**.* "Nope. This is all I have," pointing at my trusty backpack and duffle bag.

"No clothes? Nothing else?" He replies in disbelief. I just look down at my feet, unsure of the appropriate response.

"I have a couple of outfits in a locker at the Y where my friend Stacey works."

Noting my uneasiness, he quickly reassures me. "No worries. We can take care of that."

"Ella, I want to give you the key FOB to one of the Beamers. You'll need something ...er... safer...to take Ollie to preschool and run errands. You can use it whenever you want. It already has a car seat installed in the back for Ollie.

"Here are the keys to the house. The alarm code is on the key tag, but take that off after you've memorized it.

"And I picked up an American Express card for you at the bank this afternoon. I realized you'd need it since you'll be responsible for grocery shopping and supplies around the house.

"And please feel free to get yourself some clothes. I think you'll be needing more than 2 outfits. Maybe your friend Stacey can go with you on a little shopping trip."

I can't believe this is real. Not only do I get a place to sleep...inside a house...with heat...and food...and a shower... I have access to a nice car and an AMEX card. Plus, I get paid on top of all that. I must be dreaming.

"Does that sound fair, Ella?"

"More than fair Ethan. So generous."

"Well, you're going to be responsible for the most important thing in my life." He glances toward Ollie who has found a toy truck to push around the garage floor. "You need access to the things necessary to do your job."

"Ethan, I can't thank you enough."

"No need. Let's get you settled in your room."

As the three of us make our way to the door, we enter through the laundry room. Then we go into the huge, jaw-dropping kitchen. Shiny stainless-steel appliances, white marble countertops, and a huge island. A small dinette set sits cozily in the corner for informal eat-in meals.

I can't believe I'm going to cook in this kitchen. I've never seen so many cabinets and so much...of everything.

The living room and kitchen are connected in an open-concept style. There's a cozy couch in the corner facing a television. Full of toys and coloring books, a coffee table sits amidst empty juice containers and used paper plates.

Over the next hour, I lose myself in toy vehicles and pretend racing with Ollie. The hardwood floor is our racetrack with colorful toy cars spinning around the living room. As his laughter rings through the air like chimes, I can't help but be overjoyed with my new living situation.

Ethan observes from afar with a gentle smile, coffee steaming from his mug. His gaze switches between us and his work. He is a blend of parenthood and professionalism that I find unexpectedly comforting.

As night falls, the laughing in the house soothes my soul. Maybe this is the best option. Maybe this is the fresh start I so desperately need. As Ollie's giggles fade, a heaviness is lifting from my shoulders.

This isn't just a job. This is a second chance. A whole new life.

"The knights of hunger are ready to storm the castle, are they?" Ethan laughs at Oliver, who is drawing pizzas on the living room windows. I smile back, my heart pounding. He's made everything seem so normal, I've forgotten how out of place I should feel.

"Okay, pizza it is," he says, ordering on his phone. "What do you guys say? Cheese, pepperoni, or veggie?"

Oliver glances up at his father while daydreaming of a pizza castle with knights and a mote. "Peppawoni!" he shouts, making

Ethan chuckle. I start laughing when I hear his rich, honest chuckle.

I can't remember ever laughing this hard. I can't remember a day seeming this normal. This scene is unbelievable. A child's innocent laughter, a shared meal with a roof over my head in a place that already feels like home. This feels a bit alien, yet safe and hopeful.

While waiting for the pizza, Ethan and Ollie show me around the house. Probably so I don't get lost wandering around tonight.

"Hmm. We never reached your room, Ella. Follow me. You can have the guest room nearest Oliver's room. It's comfortable with a private bath and walk-in closet, that you'll soon be filling with your new clothes. I hope you know that I meant it when I said to go shopping for clothes."

We continue down the hall past Ollie's room, then Ethan's master bedroom. I only get a glance in, but it looks bigger than any apartment I've ever been in.

"At the end of the hall is the back staircase. There are four more ensuite guest rooms up there, but I thought you'd be more comfortable on the main level.

"But we can get a baby monitor to keep track of Oliver if you decide upstairs is better for you. There is an exercise gym and a theater room up there as well.

"Remember, this is now your house too, so make yourself at home and use whatever you like. Mi casa su casa."

I am flabbergasted at the reality...and enormity of the whole situation. As we make our way back to the kitchen, I am questioning if I am deserving of such a cushy set up.

Ethan watches Oliver fondly from the kitchen counter. The moment's simplicity is almost like a dream.

"So, Ella, tell me, what's your major?"

"English Literature," I say, looking at Oliver, who is drawing. "I've always been a bookworm. A world inside the pages is sometimes more pleasant than the real one."

"Ah, a fellow escapist. I get it. My love for stories is what led me to music, you know?"

"Music, huh?" I inquire. "Is it as magical as they say?"

He laughs softly, matching the room's silence. "That's one way to put it. Music is pure emotion. It's the heartbeat of life, the rhythm of existence. It transcends barriers and creates connections."

I'm lured into his passion by the image painted by his brilliant words. I'm intrigued, more than I have been in a long time.

Ethan laughs as he pushes away from the kitchen counter. "I'm actually writing a new tune. Would you like to hear it?" he asks as we return to the living room.

I settle on the couch as Oliver snuggles against my side. The room is glowing in the fading daylight. The grandfather clock ticks softly, filling the quiet.

Ethan holds a beautiful guitar, polished with a glossy finish to reflect the light. He caresses the strings, each note coaxed out gently, beautifully.

It's like seeing the artist's reverent discourse with his instrument. His fingers delicately brushing the strings. The melody twists and twirls in the air around us.

His voice is a gentle whisper, the song's words streaming off his lips. It's a heartfelt song about love and loss. His voice weaves emotion into the lyrics, tugging at something deep within me.

Oliver hops up with his bear wide-eyed and interested. He reaches for his dad's guitar. Ethan stops playing and kisses his son's forehead, smiling.

"Wanna join, buddy?" Oliver's excitement is brighter than the stars.

Hi chubby little fingers mimic his father's on the strings. Ethan guides him, their hands moving in harmony, the sound unimportant. The father-son love fills the room.

This intimate moment contrasts with the frigid loneliness of my tiny junker car. Music, joy, life. This hasn't happened in ages. I felt a part of me relax, my insecurity fading.

When the pizza arrives, Ethan breaks away from the makeshift music session to answer the door. Oliver dashes to his room and returns with a box of colorful Lego blocks. His eyes shine as he spreads them on the coffee table.

"See my castle?" He holds a half-assembled structure with a beaming smile. His pure innocence soothes my heart as I giggle at his excitement.

Under the living room lamp, laughter, music, and pizza stories fill the night. I'm hopeful for the first time in months. Pepperoni pizza and Ethan's smile while he plays Oliver's lullaby. I've been yearning for simple things like these. I finally feel noticed and included.

Tonight, I've shared a family's intimate, heartwarming scene. It's given me a sense of belonging I've craved since being adrift. As I glance around, do I dare believe things are improving?

6

KEY TO A NEW BEGINNING

ETHAN

I open my eyes to the familiar silence that typically welcomes each morning. But today is disrupted by the gurgling symphony of the coffee maker and the soft chatter of voices. My mind is reeling before reality clicks into place. Today is different. Today, Ollie and I are not alone.

I roll onto my back, scratching my eyes. I'm curious about the sounds coming from the kitchen. There's no 'wake up, Daddy!' or small feet running into my bedroom. Today is different. Today is better.

The change from solo parenthood is welcome. The cool morning air causes goosebumps as I remove the cover and glance at the clock. Late by Oliver standards, it's already 7:00.

I smell coffee as I walk down the hallway in my robe. The fragrant aroma widens my eyes. My tummy rumbles when I smell toast.

I turn the corner, pausing at the doorway to take in the view. Ella is picture perfect standing at the counter in my old college sweatshirt. Its over-sized nature engulfs her petite frame. She expertly flips French toast, the golden-brown tint indicating a perfect crisp.

Oliver is sitting on a kitchen stool, explaining his Lego palace in great detail. Ella smiles, nods along, feigning full attention to my son. My heart flutters. I've waited for this scene—my son, happy and safe, with a mother-like figure completing the picture.

As I take it all in, a strange yet familiar pang flutters in my stomach. A sensation I haven't felt since Lily died.

When I clear my throat, their heads whip around simultaneously. Oliver smiles, nearly falling off his stool with his morning eagerness. Ella glances at me with her bright green eyes. Eyes that can engulf me. Her cheeks are pink, either from cooking or embarrassment, I'm not sure which.

"Daddy! Ella made me toast! She even cut it into little triangles like you!" His exuberance fills the room, making me chuckle. Ella looks at me, a little unsure.

Shaking off the final remnants of my sleep, I walk over to them. I ruffle Oliver's hair, then turn to Ella, hoping my eyes reflect thanks and comfort. "Ella, thank you. I'm delighted someone finally got this early bird to change his wake-up call."

Breakfast is a simple affair, filled with Oliver's stories. Tales of Lego conquests absorbed through Ella's quiet amusement. I chat more about my music, share snippets of songs I'm working on, and listen to Ella's thoughtful insights.

Today is different for the first time in ages. I'm Ethan again today, Oliver's father. I'm a man sharing his home, his son, his life with someone who cares. I sense normalcy for the first time in a long time.

"Oh, this...I found it in the guest room," Ella stammers, tugging at my old sweatshirt hem. She twisted the fabric nervously around her fingers, her cheeks flaming red. "I'll do laundry later today...if that's okay?"

I snicker at her silly inquiry. "Ella, it's fine. You don't have to ask. You're not a guest. That is your room, no longer a guest room. Feel free to make yourself at home."

My words make her shoulders relax and her lips smile. Warmth replaces tension in the room.

We laugh at Oliver's eager account of the Lego knight's war. His words rush out in a fury; the syrup from his French toast has him on a sugar high.

"You know, Ella," I begin, turning towards her as I rinse a plate, "Oliver usually goes to preschool during the day. When do you have class?"

Ella reaches to take the plate from me, and our hands momentarily occupy the same area of the plate. We both freeze, our eyes locked. As I release the plate into her hands, I note the electric sensation I feel when her hand touched mine.

What was that? NO. Can't be. She didn't feel anything. Ella continues without hesitation.

"I have class on Monday, Tuesday and Thursday mornings, but I usually study in the library the other days."

"I see. Well, on Tuesdays and Thursdays, you can drop Oliver off at pre-school. That way I can go in later as I only have afternoon office hours on those days. On the other days, we can ride in together unless you have other plans. How does that sound?"

"That's fine. Anything's fine. Remember...I've been living in my car, so I was always on campus with nothing else to do but study. This is a welcome change of obligations."

I release a breath I hadn't realized I'd been holding, grateful for her acceptance. We finish cleaning up in silence, the steady rhythm of our movements echoing in the room.

"Saturdays are typically 'Dad days' for Ollie and me. At least I try as much as possible to spend the whole day with him.

"We've been planning a trip to the children's science museum for today and I hate to disappoint him. After you've been here for a while, I'm sure we will want you to come along, but I hope you don't mind giving us this day together."

Ella nods, understanding evident in her eyes. "Of course," she agrees, her voice steady. "I wouldn't expect anything less."

Once we're done, Oliver races off to get ready for the children's museum, leaving Ella and me in the kitchen. We stand there, a safe distance apart, the hum of the refrigerator the only sound in the room. It feels comfortable, familiar.

"Ella," I start, looking at her earnestly, "I can't thank you enough for this—for helping me out, for being here with Oliver. I want you to know that I'm here if you need anything."

She looks at me, her green eyes soft. "Thank you, Ethan," she says, her voice gentle. "I appreciate that."

As I watch her turn to leave the room, a strange sensation grips me—a mixture of relief, hope, and a hint of something more. I can't put a finger on it, but I decide to let it be. For now, all that matters is that Ella is here. And somehow, in this beautiful, chaotic mess of life, everything feels just right.

7

THE EXCURSIONS

ELLA

After Ethan and Ollie leave for the museum, I realize how right Ethan is. I need more than 2 outfits...especially since they're both at the Y. So I decide to text Stacey.

Hey! Are you working today?

(Stacey) No. I've been waiting
to hear from you.
I was sure you had been sold
into slavery by the
human trafficker.

**Very funny Stace.
It couldn't be more awesome.
Wanna go shopping
with me this afternoon?**

(Stacey) WHAT? How's that going to work?
But sure! I'll bite.

**Great! Meet me at
the Y in 30 minutes.
I need to get my stuff
out of the locker.**

(Stacey) *Got it!*

I grab my backpack and head for the garage. I can't bring myself to drive Ethan's BMW, so I get in my heap of scrap metal and head to the Y.

Stacey is already there when I arrive. "Here you go. I went ahead and cleaned out your locker. Hope you don't mind."

"Of course not. Can you drive? I have to tell you all about the Hartley Manor." Stacey's confused look says it all. My totally perplexing situation. Yesterday my friend had to buy my lunch and today I am shopping for clothes with my boss's AMEX card!

After a very frugal shopping excursion, Stacey drives us back to the Y to get my car. I'm not quite done talking the situation through with my friend, so I stay in the car to talk longer.

"Do you think I bought too much Stace?"

"Are you kidding? You barely bought anything. Some underwear, a nightgown and a couple pair of jeans. I would have gone hog wild if I were you!"

"And 3 new blouses. I just don't want Ethan to think I'm going to bilk him right off the bat. I'll get more when I feel a little more comfortable."

"Sure. Right after you get brave enough to drive his Beamer?"

"Well, I'll have to drive it whenever I take Ollie anywhere. I clearly cannot fit a car seat in my hunk-a-junk. But whatever...Do you think Ethan is good looking?"

"Well, I just saw him briefly in the coffee shop yesterday. Yes, I was stalking you. I had to see for myself that you weren't in danger. But yes, I think he's attractive. Why? Do you have a crush on your boss after one day?" she taunts.

"Cut it out Stacey. I'm being serious. Every time he is close to me, I can't catch my breath and I get butterflies in my belly. What's up with that?"

"Well just how close has he been to you?" she says accusingly.

"Not like that close or anything. Just standing...you know...in the same vicinity...I get a funny feeling. When our hands touched as we were doing the dishes, I felt like I couldn't breathe. But he didn't seem to notice anything, so I went on with what I was doing.

"Maybe I'm feeling a sense of acceptance? I haven't felt like part of anything for a very long time."

"Yeah. That's probably it, Ella. You sound like you really like little Oliver and he is taking to you well. You've just forgotten how it feels to be a welcomed part of something."

"Yeah...I know you're right...it just...feels different somehow."

―――ele―――

ETHAN

I stand back and watch as Ollie listens intently to the museum guide at the dinosaur exhibit. It's Ollie's favorite because he gets to search for dinosaur bones after the talk.

The toddlers each get a plastic bucket and a paint brush. They are turned loose in the sand box and are taught to brush away the sand to discover and collect the hidden dinosaur bones.

My phone buzzes. I should've known I would get a text from Alice today. Predictable.

(Alice) Well how did last night go?

Okay I guess.

(Alice) Just okay? What happened?

**Nothing. Ella's been settling in.
I think Ollie really likes her.
He thinks she's his special friend.**

(Alice) That's great. How do you like her?

**She's doing a great job so far.
Made breakfast,
cleaned up the mess.**

(Alice) That's an improvement
over you and Ollie.

**I think she feels
like a fish out of water.**

(Alice) But I bet she'll fit in fine
after she relaxes a little.

**Maybe.
Thanks for sending her to us.**

After texting with Alice, I start thinking about Ella and the feeling I got when our hands touched. *Am I making way more out of this than it really is? She's not the type to fall for a college professor. Or is she?*

8

Monday, Monday

ETHAN

Our first weekday since Ella's been with us. I hope the craziness of our life doesn't scare Ella away. Hopefully her presence will eliminate a lot of the chaos. How nice it will be to share some of life's dilemmas with another adult person.

I must be sure not to ask too much of her, especially this first week. She needs to feel at home here.

Ella's voice pulls me from my thoughts. "Ethan," she says, her tone uncertain. "I... um, my class is canceled today, so I was wondering if I could... you know, stay here."

There's a vulnerability in her eyes, a faint plea for understanding that grips my heart. There's something about her voice. Something comforting that instills a sense of trust in me.

Perhaps it's the sincerity in her eyes. Or the gentle nature of her disposition. Or simply the way she's fit into our lives as if she's always belonged. Whatever it is, it compels me to take a leap of faith.

"Yeah, of course, Ella," I respond, my voice steady. Just make yourself at home."

Before either of us can say anything else, a small voice pipes up. "Daddy, do I have to go to school now?" Oliver asks, his eyes wide and hopeful. "I wanna play with Ella."

His words hang in the air, heavy with an innocence. It's both endearing and heart-wrenching. I can't help but chuckle at his enthusiasm, my heart swelling with affection for my little boy.

"Well, buddy," I say, bending down to his level, "Ella will still be here when you get back from school. You can play with her all evening, okay?"

His face lights up at my words, his eyes sparkling with anticipation. "Really?" he asks, his voice filled with awe.

Before I can respond, he's already rushing over to Ella, throwing his arms around her in a tight hug.

Ella goes down on her knees to meet his embrace. Her arms wrap around him with a tenderness that leaves me speechless. Their bond, strong and genuine, blossoms right before my eyes. It's a beautiful testament to the magic of unexpected friendships.

As I watch them, I can't help but think that maybe, just maybe, this was what we needed all along. Ella's presence in our lives is a beacon of light. To bring us a sense of normalcy, comfort, and an overwhelming amount of joy.

It's a new day, a new beginning, the golden glow of the morning. I watch as my son and our new friend share a moment of pure, unadulterated happiness. It's simple, it's raw, and it's perfect. And for the first time in a long while, I find myself looking forward to what the future holds for us.

The drive to Oliver's preschool is filled with light chatter and the steady rhythm of Oliver's favorite songs. As we pull up to the school, my heart flutters at the sight of his excitement.

With his Spiderman lunchbox and a backpack almost bigger than him, he springs out of the car with a barely suppressed grin on his face. I walk him to the classroom door and wave at Miss Jennifer.

"Bye, Daddy," he calls over his shoulder, waving at me with an energy that seems endless. I wave back and watch as he disappears into the room with an eagerness that reminds me of my own childhood.

I return to the car and head toward the university. The morning sun beams through the car windows, casting a warm glow on the dash. I drive through the streets I've memorized over the years and take all the familiar turns.

Arriving at the university, I park in my usual spot, feeling the comfortable routine of it all set in. It's a day like any other, filled with lectures, discussions, and laughter. Yet there's a different kind of energy in the air today, a hopeful hum that I can't quite put my finger on. But I welcome it.

ETHAN

Once my work for the day is done, I collect my belongings and head back to my car. As I slide into the driver's seat, a small, almost unnoticed, pang of anticipation fills me.

I'm eager to return home, eager to see Oliver, and surprisingly, eager to see Ella. It's a strange feeling, a new feeling, but not an unwelcome one.

The drive to the preschool seems quicker than normal. As I arrive, I can see Oliver from a distance, waiting patiently on the steps, his eyes scanning the horizon for my car. When he spots me, his face breaks into the widest grin, his small hand waving with a frantic cadence.

After I park and start up the walk, "Daddy!" He runs full speed to me and I catch him in my arms, lifting him up in a tight hug.

"Did you have a good day, buddy?" I ask as I settle him in the back seat.

He's quick to share every detail of his day, his words tumbling over each other in a rush to be heard. As we drive home, I listen to his stories, his giggles, and his enthusiastic tales of playground politics and art class masterpieces.

Pulling into the driveway, our house comes into view. It's the same place I've seen every day, but today, it feels different. It feels warmer, brighter, more inviting than ever before.

"Let's park out front today so we can surprise Ella."

As we walk through the front door, my senses are immediately drawn to the change in the house. It's not only the absence of scattered toys and strewn laundry that Oliver and I had grown so accustomed to. No, it's more than that.

It's the unmistakable freshness in the air. The gleaming surfaces, and the faint scent of lavender. It's the silence that no longer echoes with loneliness but is filled with the quiet hum of contentment.

And there, at the center of this transformation, stands Ella. Her hair, still slightly damp from a recent shower, hangs loosely around her shoulders. Her face catching the evening light streaming in from the windows.

She's changed into a new pair of jeans and a soft flowing shirt that subtly accentuates the curves of her slender form. There's a renewed vitality in her eyes. A brightness that wasn't there before, mirroring the radiant smile on her face.

"Hi! Welcome, Ollie!" She bends down to greet Ollie first, opening her arms wide. His little body launches into her embrace. His laughter ringing through the house as she spins him around.

"Ella!" He squeals in delight, his voice filled with genuine affection.

Once she sets him down, her gaze turns toward me, her welcoming smile still intact. "Hi, Ethan. Welcome home. I...I prepared some dinner for us -- I hope you don't mind." Her voice is soft, a touch uncertain, as if she's not sure how her initiative would be received.

But as the aroma of cooked food saturates the air, my stomach grumbles in response. I can't help but let out a chuckle. "Mind?" I shake my head, inhaling deeply. "My stomach would beg to differ. It smells incredible, Ella."

A light blush dusts her cheeks, and she ducks her head to hide her growing smile. "Oh, it was nothing. It felt good to finally cook in a real house, in a real kitchen."

For a moment, I look at her, struggling with a mixture of gratitude and an attraction toward Ella I can't explain. It's her warmth and her kindness that somehow feels like a soothing balm to my weathered heart.

"Thank you, Ella," I manage to say, my voice carrying more weight than the two simple words usually do.

For a moment, she looks up, her eyes meeting mine. There's an understanding and acknowledgement that she's brought life back into our home. A life that Oliver and I didn't realize we were missing until she walked through our door.

The day ends not with a grand fanfare but with small moments stitched together by Ella's kindness. We share a meal, trade stories, and bask in the novelty of a newfound friendship. The house, once a lonely solitude, is now filled with laughter and conversations and life.

And as I lie in bed that night, the house quiet once again, I realize something. It's not the cleanliness or the food or the company that's different. It's the feeling of home that Ella has brought with her, a feeling that had faded away without my notice.

But now, it's back, stronger and more profound than ever before. And for the first time in a long while, I fall asleep not to the rhythm of silence but to the sound of a home revived.

9

A Feminine Touch

ETHAN

There's something about the soft humming of the morning that rouses me awake. The house, usually quiet and drab, is alive with subtle energy. A feminine touch. I roll over on the bed and let my eyes adjust to the morning sunlight filtering through the blinds.

I smell the faint aroma of breakfast. A combination of eggs and bacon that's making my stomach grumble in anticipation.

Pulling back the covers, I swing my legs over the side of the bed. I stand, stretching to relieve the stiffness in my muscles. I make my way out of the bedroom, following the delicious smell towards the kitchen.

The sight that greets me almost makes my heart stop.

Ella is there, moving around with ease and grace, her hair tied up in a messy bun that adds to her allure. She's wearing a short skirt, the fabric barely reaching her mid-thighs.

As she bends over slightly to flip the bacon, I catch a glimpse of her pink thong. My throat runs dry, and for a moment, my mind goes blank.

What am I thinking? Oh my...

I try to tear my gaze away, but my eyes have a mind of their own, feasting on her beautiful legs that seem to go on forever. I remind myself to breathe. I have to shake my head to clear the fog of desire that's clouding my thoughts.

It's been a few weeks since Ella moved in, and things have improved immensely around here. The house feels warmer, livelier, a stark contrast to how it used to be. I guess, a woman's touch does make everything better.

"Good morning!" She greets me cheerfully, her voice pulling me out of my thoughts. She glances over her shoulder, her eyes meeting mine. There's a sparkle in them that takes my breath away. Her lips curve into a soft smile, and my heart skips a beat.

"Morning, Ella." I manage to reply, clearing my throat.

She turns back to the stove, flipping the bacon with expertise. A few minutes later, she places a plate in front of me. The eggs are cooked perfectly, the yolks still runny, and the bacon is crispy, just the way I like it.

I watch as she flits around the kitchen, tending to Ollie's breakfast next. Her movements fluid and graceful, like a dance she's known all her life.

Despite the sudden surge of unspoken desire, I can't deny that having her here feels so right. A feeling I haven't felt in a long time, a feeling that makes me hope for more.

The morning seems to slide into afternoon with ease. Ella's presence is a soothing constant as we navigate through the day. There's a rhythm to our shared existence, a dance that we're both learning step by step. Ollie is at his happiest, his laughter a background melody that brightens our day.

But beneath the calmness, there's an unmistakable tension. A growing connection, a smoldering fire that threatens to consume us both. We're both circling around it, too cautious and too aware of the potential destruction that might follow.

We find ourselves alone in the kitchen, the dishes from lunch scattered around. I remind Ella that we have a dishwasher, but she insists on washing them herself. A dishwasher is something she grew up without, so she prefers not to use it. Someday she'll change her mind…maybe.

Ella is washing and I am drying, a routine we fell into without words. Her skirt sways as she moves, her toned legs and tiny waist captivating me. I can't tear my gaze away, my mind filled with thoughts I know I shouldn't entertain.

"Can you hand me that plate, Ethan?" Her voice breaks into my reverie, and I quickly pass her the plate. Our fingers brush ever so slightly in the exchange.

The contact again sends a shock of electricity through me, my pulse racing. There's an undeniable chemistry between us. One that we've been tiptoeing around for days. Her breath hitches at the touch, her eyelashes fluttering as she lifts her gaze to meet mine. Her lips part slightly, a rosy hue spreading across her cheeks.

I'm overly aware of her soft floral scent that's uniquely hers. It wraps around me, a sweet torture that leaves me yearning for more. My hand is still hovering in the air, the tingling sensation of her touch fresh in my mind. My heart pounds in my chest, and I can't help but wonder if she can hear it too.

She swallows hard, the sound seeming to echo in the silence. The look in her eyes is intoxicating. It's filled with confusion, desire, and something else. Something that makes my heart flutter with anticipation.

We stand there, locked in a moment that feels suspended in time. The intensity of our gaze, unspoken words that hang in the air, a confession too early to acknowledge.

There's a war within me. A battle between the logical part of my brain and the raw, visceral attraction that's pulling me towards her.

"Ella…" I begin, my voice but a whisper. I want to say something, anything, to break this spell, to regain control over the situation.

But then, Ollie's laughter resonates from the living room, and we both flinch, the spell broken. Ella averts her eyes, her cheeks flaming. She mutters a quick "excuse me" and rushes out of the kitchen. She leaves me standing in the middle of the room, her scent still lingering around me.

Her absence creates a deafening silence. I can't help but notice my fingertips are still tingling from the contact.

A part of me knows that this is dangerous territory, a road that we shouldn't venture down. But another part of me, a part that's been dormant for so long, yearns for the promise of something more.

With a sigh, I turn back to the dishes, the question of what comes next heavy in my mind. The tension, the desire, the undeniable connection... it's all there, simmering right beneath the surface. But for now, it remains unspoken, a secret shared between two guarded hearts.

It's Saturday and our 'Dad Day' has already become a family day. We decide to visit the local aquarium. Ollie's insatiable fascination with marine life provides a perfect escape from the norm. Ella's excitement mirrors Ollie's. Her eyes sparkling with anticipation as we pull into the parking lot.

"Look, Ollie, that's the largest tank over there," Ella points out. As we enter the expansive aquarium, her voice is brimming with infectious enthusiasm. Ollie's eyes widen at the sight of the deep blue water. It's teeming with vibrant, colorful creatures of all shapes and sizes.

The aquarium is bathed in soft, refracted light. It lends an almost ethereal quality to the space. The serene quiet is punctuated only by the muted bubbling of water. And the occasional exclamations of wonder from visitors.

Guiding Ollie by the hand, Ella leads us through the labyrinth of tanks. Each holds a unique spectacle of the underwater world.

Her profile is illuminated by the soft glow of the tanks, casting her in a beautiful, dreamlike light. The sight takes my breath away, and I can't help but watch. Her excitement, her joy, the way she interacts with Ollie - with a sense of wonder.

In front of a particularly large tank, Ollie squeals in delight. He's pointing at a school of vibrant clownfish darting among the anemones. Ella squats down to his level, tracing the path of the fish with her finger on the glass to help him follow.

"See, Ollie, these are clownfish. They have a special relationship with the anemones," Ella explains. Her tone is patient and filled with warmth. Ollie nods along, drinking in her every word.

We continue our journey through the oceanic world. Our path is illuminated by the glow of jellyfish. The scales of the tuna and the graceful dance of the sea turtles create an exciting atmosphere. It all piques Ollie's interest and enthusiasm. Never fading, his laughter and chatter echoing in the cavernous space.

As we reach the end of our tour, Ollie's excitement spikes at the sight of the penguin exhibit. His laughter and joyful exclamations are music to my ears, a testament to the joy this day has brought him.

Ella and I exchange a glance over his head, a shared moment of contentment that warms me from the inside out.

The bustle of the aquarium pales as an elderly lady meanders towards us. She is leaning on a cane and arm in arm with her companion. Her eyes crinkle at the corners, a lifetime of laughter and joy etched in the fine lines on her face. She bestows upon us a warm smile that instantly disarms me.

"Oh, what a beautiful couple," she coos, her gaze flitting between Ella, Ollie, and me. Her words hang in the air, the three of us frozen in that moment.

A normal reaction might have been to clarify, to point out the misunderstanding. But before I can muster a response, Ella saves the moment.

"Thank you so much," she says, her voice a soft trill that fills the space between us. I see the corners of her mouth curling upwards in a genuine smile. Her eyes sparkle with some unreadable emotion.

Caught off guard, I feel Ella snuggling closer to me, and without thinking, I slide my arm around her waist. It's a natural movement, one that doesn't feel forced or out of place. Her body fits perfectly against mine.

Her warmth seeps through the thin fabric of her shirt and into my skin. Her sweet scent - a mix of her shampoo and something distinctly hers - fills my nostrils and clouds my thoughts.

My hand rests on the curve of her waist, the sensation of her against me, stoking a low heat in my belly. A sudden rush of desire hits me, raw and powerful, like a dormant beast awakening within. Her body stiffens at the contact, and then relaxes as she leans further into my embrace.

The world around us fades away, replaced by the feeling of Ella against me. Her soft breath on my skin and the smell of her hair. I look down, her eyes wide and innocent, her cheeks a light pink. My heartbeat quickens, a rush of blood roaring in my ears, drowning out the noise of the aquarium.

The tension between us is a living entity, thrumming with a life of its own. It wraps around us like a cocoon, separating us from the world outside. My grip tightens on her waist involuntarily, my body reacting on its own accord.

My mind is a whirlpool of emotions - surprise, confusion. But most of all, a smoldering desire, growing with each second that I hold her close.

The world snaps back into focus when Ollie tugs on my hand, eager to explore more of the aquarium. Ella steps back, the absence of her warmth like a physical blow. She sends me a small smile before diverting her attention back to Ollie.

But as we continue our exploration, the spark that ignited between us remains. It's lingering in the air, in my thoughts, in the space where our bodies just met. And as I steal glances at her throughout the rest of our visit, I can't help but wonder - did she feel it too?

10

A Symphony of Unplayed Notes

ELLA

I'm curled up on the couch with one arm wrapped protectively around Ollie. My other hand absentmindedly traces patterns on the cushion. The soft glow of the lamp illuminates the room, casting a warm, homely feel.

The shadows dance on the walls as the gentle thrum of Ethan's guitar strings fill the room. It's these moments that I cherish the most. These quiet evenings where time seems to halt, and life narrows down to only the three of us.

Weeks have passed since I moved into their house. I can say with certainty that I didn't just find a place to stay, I found a home.

It's in the way Ethan and Ollie welcome me each day. In the way we navigate around each other in the kitchen during breakfast chaos. In the way we've crafted small but significant rituals that bind us together.

Ollie's head is heavy against my thigh, his soft curls tickling my skin through my jeans. His eyelids are growing heavy.

The energetic spark that usually shines in his hazel eyes are dimming. The lullaby of Ethan's music soothes him into sleep.

A wave of affection crashes over me as I watch him fight the pull of sleep. His little body grows limp with each passing second.

Across the room, Ethan sits with his guitar in his hands, lost in his music. His eyes are closed, his long fingers moving fluidly across the guitar strings. Each note echoes his deep, soulful connection with the melody he creates.

It's a side of Ethan I've come to appreciate, the passionate musician who becomes one with his music. The soft lines of his face are relaxed. His chest rises and falls rhythmically with the tempo. The peaceful aura around him filling the room.

As the final notes of the song dissipate into the quiet evening, I look down to find Ollie fast asleep. His little chest rises and falls steadily, his mouth slightly open as he breathes softly.

I gently untangle myself from him, my movements slow and deliberate so as not to wake him. Carefully, I lift his head and slide a soft pillow under it. His face scrunches up momentarily before relaxing again. His tiny fingers curling around the edge of the pillow.

Looking back up, I meet Ethan's gaze. He has been watching us, his expression soft. There's an unspoken appreciation in his eyes, a silent thank you that makes my heart flutter. I offer him a small smile, nodding toward Ollie.

Ethan rises from his chair, placing his guitar gently on its stand, and walks over to us. He kneels beside Ollie, his hand reaching out to brush a few stray curls off his son's face.

There's so much love in that simple gesture, so much warmth. I have a strange sense of belonging, a feeling I haven't felt in a long time.

Life here is not perfect. We have our chaos, our occasional messes, our disagreements. But every night I sit here listening to Ethan's music, with Ollie snuggled up to me.

He's falling asleep to the rhythm of our heartbeats, and I know I wouldn't trade this for anything else in the world. This is our little slice of heaven, our safe place, our home. And I'm grateful to be a part of it.

The black grand piano in the sitting room has always caught my attention. The large instrument sits regally in one corner of the adjoining room. Its lacquered surface gleams in the soft light.

It's a stark contrast to the lived-in coziness of the rest of the room, an untouched relic of the past. But for all its grandeur, I've never seen Ethan play it.

"I've never seen you play that piano," I mention casually, motioning toward the piano with a nod of my head. Ethan's gaze follows my gesture, settling on the silent instrument.

"Yeah…" he begins, a hint of melancholy seeping into his voice. He pauses, gathering his thoughts before continuing. "That belonged to my late wife, Lily." His tone is matter of fact and void of any bitterness. But there's weight to his words, a glimpse into the past that he's rarely shared.

A pang of regret washes over me. I didn't mean to pry. "Oh, Ethan, I... I'm sorry, I didn't mean to..." I stumble over my words, uncertain of how to tread this delicate territory.

He waves a hand dismissively, a reassuring smile spreading across his face. "It's fine, Ella. Really." His voice holds no trace of resentment or discomfort. Instead, it's laced with a subtle warmth, reflecting the acceptance of a loss long past.

A moment of silence stretches between us. The quiet of the room accentuates the gravity of the conversation. I glance at him, observing the stoic set of his jaw, the gentle hardness in his gaze. I admire his strength, his ability to share his pain so openly.

Without warning, his lips twitch into a small smile. "You know," he starts, breaking the silence. "I've actually been looking for an excuse to play it again. If you want, I can show you some basic stuff."

"Sure," I reply, excitement bubbling up within me. The thought of him playing the piano and learning a few chords myself is thrilling. I move over to the piano, the cool wooden bench chilling through my jeans as I sit down.

Ethan joins me, his body radiating warmth as he settles next to me. The distance between us is minimal, our shoulders nearly brushing, but it's relaxed. Natural.

The comfortable silence between us settles like a soft blanket. It envelops us in a shared experience as Ethan lifts the piano's polished lid. A faint echo resonates in the room, the promise of melodies that are yet to fill the silence.

His hands move with a graceful sureness over the ivory keys. It's telling of the music he's capable of playing, evident in every gesture. I watch, captivated, each note striking a chord in my heart.

With a light clearing of his throat, Ethan shifts his gaze towards me, an easy grin playing on his lips. "Here, let me show you," he offers, his voice a gentle murmur. Slowly, he reaches over, his warm fingers brushing against my cooler ones. It sends a jolt of electricity up my arm.

My heart picks up pace, pounding in rhythm with the anticipation building in the air. His hand, strong and warm, engulfs mine. Gently guiding it to the correct position on the keys, it's a simple touch. Innocent, and yet it ignites a spark within me.

I can feel the rough pads of his fingertips against my own. The callouses born from years of strumming the guitar strings. His touch is reassuring, grounding, a silent promise of support and guidance.

We're seated so close now that I can feel the warmth radiating off him, a comforting presence in the chilly room. His scent fills my senses. An intoxicating mix of citrus and woodsy undertones has my head swimming.

I find myself leaning into him unknowingly, drawn by the magnetic pull he seems to have over me. With a gentle nudge, he prompts my fingers into action, guiding them to press on the correct keys.

His chest rises and falls rhythmically beside me. The steady cadence is somehow soothing. His firm grip around my hand never falters. It provides a secure anchor in this new and exciting territory.

"Ella, you're doing great." Ethan's husky whisper seems to caress my ear. His words resonate within the close quarters between us. His breath, warm and minty, tickles my skin, making my pulse quicken.

His reassurances paint a serene backdrop against our hushed surroundings. My senses key into every word, every caress of air, each vibration of his voice.

"I... I'm trying." I stutter, feeling the warmth of his body next to mine. My concentration is torn from the keys under our hands by his captivating presence. He chuckles softly. His lips part into a warm, encouraging smile that somehow seems more intimate than any touch.

"Remember, it's just you and the music. Let it take you," he murmurs, his voice soothing like the gentle hum of a lullaby. His free hand rests at the small of my back. It becomes a stabilizing presence. His other hand continues to guide my fingers, instilling confidence in me with every note.

The world shrinks down to only us. I'm hyper-aware of every minor shift, every tiny sigh he makes, each whisper of cloth as he shifts beside me. Our closeness is dizzying. His scent, his warmth, the low rumble of his voice. Everything about Ethan becomes my entire world in this moment.

An unexpected wave of boldness washes over me, spurred on by the trusting ambiance he's cocooned us in. Turning to face him, our eyes meet, and something unspoken passes between us. His gaze softens, the usual spark in his eyes giving way to a warm, glowing ember.

We lean towards each other, in an achingly slow motion. His hand loosens from mine, instead coming to rest on my cheek, his thumb gently tracing the curve of my jaw. His touch sends a shiver coursing through me, pooling a warm sensation in my stomach.

Our breaths mingle, my heart pounding in my chest as the space between us diminishes. Our faces are mere inches apart, and I can see the flecks of gold in his green eyes, sparkling under the ambient light.

His gaze drops to my lips, lingering there, and then flicks back up to my eyes. I can almost taste the mint on his breath as he leans closer, our noses brushing. The world falls away, leaving only the two of us suspended in this single, electrifying moment.

But just as his lips are a hairbreadth away from mine, a piercing cry from the living room shatters the charged silence. Our eyes flit open, instantly breaking the spell.

Ollie. Ethan immediately pulls away, concern etched on his features. "Ollie must've had a nightmare," he mutters, quickly standing and rushing to his son's aid.

I'm left there, with my heart pounding. My skin tingling from the almost-kiss, a symphony of unplayed notes hanging in the air between us.

11

THE ELEPHANT IN THE ROOM

ETHAN

In the quiet solitude of my room, I lay staring at the ceiling, my thoughts consumed by Ella. Her. The young woman who, over the weeks, had begun to fill up spaces in my life and heart that I hadn't known were empty.

Tonight, the image of our near kiss keeps replaying in my mind like a movie stuck on loop. I can't help but wonder - did I cross a line? The rhythm of my heart syncopates with the memory of her lips, so close to mine.

A dull, almost painful longing tugs at my chest. The memory of her touch, her smell, her taste right on the tip of my tongue, yet so cruelly denied. The softness of her hand, the delicate fragrance of her hair, the look in her eyes. All painting a tantalizing picture that keeps me awake.

My mind is awash with the memory of her fingers beneath mine on the ivory keys. Her slight intake of breath as our hands brushed. The way her eyes had widened in surprise and... something else. Desire? No, it couldn't be.

I remember her nervous laughter, the blush that crept up her cheeks. The way her chest rose and fell with every breath she took. The memory of her warm touch, and the soft fabric of her shirt brushing against my arm. It's all too much and not enough at the same time.

The scent of her lingers in my senses, a mix of fresh flowers and a hint of the vanilla-scented shampoo she uses. It had wrapped around me when we were so close, invading my senses, making me yearn for her even more.

God, her lips. They had been mere inches away, plump and so inviting, a sweet temptation that I'd barely resisted. Would they be as soft as they looked? What would her lips taste like? Would they taste as sweet as the homemade peach pie she made last week? I find myself yearning to know.

The regret of not bridging the final gap, of not pressing my lips to hers when I had the chance, gnaws at me. The urge to know the feel of her lips against mine is a throbbing undercurrent. A wave threatening to pull me under.

But then doubt creeps in. What if I misread the signals? What if she didn't want the kiss as much as I did? What if our close encounter on the piano bench was only a friendly gesture and nothing more?

I groan, rubbing my face with my hands, the cotton of my pillowcase rough under my fingers. This is all too much. I need sleep, but every time I close my eyes, her face swims into view. The phantom feeling of her touch on my skin resurfaces, and I'm wide awake again.

It's going to be a long night.

The night is silent, the only sound is the faint chirping of crickets from outside. The illuminated screen of my phone reads 2:11 am. Sleep, it seems, is an elusive entity tonight. I decide to head to the kitchen, hoping that a glass of warm milk might soothe my unsettled mind.

As I make my way down the dimly lit hallway in my boxers, the faint glow from the living room catches my eye. Ella. She's curled up on the couch, engrossed in some rom-com flickering on the television screen. The volume low enough not to disturb the tranquility of the night.

"Ella?" I whisper, not wanting to startle her. She turns, a soft smile appearing on her face. The sight of her in the dim light makes my heart pound harder against my ribcage. She looks stunning, even with her hair tousled and eyes glassy from the lack of sleep.

"I couldn't sleep," I admit, rubbing the back of my neck in a futile attempt to diffuse the tension coiling within me.

"Neither could I." Her gaze holds mine with an intensity that sends a jolt of electricity down my spine.

"You hungry?" she blurts, interrupting my train of thought. "I noticed you hardly touched your dinner. The leftovers are in the fridge if you want."

With that, she stands, crossing the distance to the kitchen island. She takes a plate of leftovers from the refrigerator and places it in the microwave. I watch her, entranced by the movements of her bare feet padding against the cold tiles.

Her silhouette glows against the dim lights of the kitchen. She's irresistible, a tantalizing mystery that I find myself drawn to more and more each day.

"Thanks, Ella," I manage to mutter, as she places the reheated food in front of me at the dinette table. It's all I can do to keep my eyes from straying, from drinking in the sight of her, but it's a losing battle.

There's an undercurrent of something more. Something potent and magnetic tugs at us both. It's the elephant in the room, the 'almost' moment from earlier that we've been tiptoeing around.

The lingering ghost of our almost kiss weaves an invisible thread between us. It fills the air with an undeniable tension that neither of us can ignore anymore.

She takes the seat closest to me and I watch as she tucks a loose strand of hair behind her ear. Her gaze focuses on some distant point. I'm curious if she's as affected by this as I am.

Taking a deep breath, I decide to face the inevitable. The silence of the night, the shared insomnia, our electrifying encounter earlier, and now this... It's all leading to something.

Something that, despite my initial resistance, I find myself wanting, needing to explore. And the first step is to acknowledge it. The connection, the tension, the unspoken desire that has been simmering between us. It's time to face the music.

"About earlier..." I start, my voice just above a whisper, but loud enough in the quiet of the night. I see her body stiffen, and I know I've got her attention.

She looks at me, her green eyes shimmering with something unreadable. "What about it?" Her voice is filled with a curiosity. She is not oblivious to the obvious attraction between us.

The words that had been lodged in my throat finally escape in a soft whisper. "Ella... did you... I mean, were we...were we actually about to... kiss?" I stumble through the words, my gaze never leaving her face. "Did I cross a line I shouldn't have? I didn't...I couldn't..."

The room grows eerily quiet for a moment, the tension building to an almost unbearable degree. Her eyes are locked onto mine.

Without a word, she turns and gracefully lowers herself onto my lap, straddling me with her legs. Her weight settles on me, and I take a deep breath, taking in the intoxicating scent of her hair.

12

THE SUBMISSION

ETHAN

Her lips part, and with a sensual breath, she confesses, "Yes, I thought we were about to kiss." The words hang between us, charged with a fiery passion that ignites every inch of my being.

Her arms wrap around my neck, pulling me in closer. I can feel her heart beating as fast as mine as she whispers, "And it was a line I wanted you to cross." Then she closes the gap, her lips pressing against mine with a fervor that takes my breath away.

The kiss is intense, her lips moving against mine in a fierce and passionate dance. It leaves no room for doubts or uncertainties. It's as if a dam has burst within me, all my pent-up emotions spilling out, making me kiss her back with an equal intensity.

Her fingers run through my hair, pulling me closer, while her other hand traces down my chest. Her touch leaves a trail of fire in its wake.

She's intoxicating. The taste of her lips, the scent of her skin, and the feel of her body against mine creating a heady mix of desire. An exhilaration that leaves me wanting more.

I reciprocate the intensity of her kiss. One hand cups her cheek, the other winds around her waist to bring her closer. She fits perfectly against me. Like two pieces of a jigsaw puzzle that had been searching for each other all along.

The connection is undeniable. A magnetic force that pulls us closer, making us lose ourselves in the shared heat of the moment.

Her mouth moves against mine in a rhythm that speaks of a desire as raw and primal as the one burning within me. It's an exploration, a dance, a battle, and a surrender all at once. I pull her closer, the feel of her body flush against mine only fueling my desire for her.

The oversized shirt she's wearing leaves her curves exposed. I slide my hand up her back then around to the front to feel her breast, so full, so firm. I twist her nipple then trace around it, brushing it with my finger.

I can feel my cock growing harder with each passing moment. I can feel her wetness, and I realize that she is not wearing any panties. The realization only intensifies my hunger for her. I want to explore every inch of her body, to taste her, to fuck her.

She's irresistible, and I know that I need her now. I reach between her legs feeling her wetness with my thumb. Her body tenses and I hear her gasp in pleasure. I continue to tease her with my fingers, I can feel her growing more and more desperate to go farther.

Her hips start to move against my hand in a frenzied rhythm, and I know that she's close. But I'm not quite ready to let her go yet. I slow down my movements, teasing her with a light touch that only grazes her clit.

She lets out a frustrated whimper, her hands moving to grip my shoulders. I can feel her nails digging into my skin, and I know that she's about to lose control.

I continue to tease her, my movements light and taunting. "I need you," she whispers, her voice barely above a breath. "Please, I can't take it anymore."

With a sudden and firm touch, I plunge my fingers inside her, my movements quick and unrelenting. She cries out, her body writhing against mine. It's a beautiful sight, her body trembling and pulsing with pleasure, and I know that I'll never get enough of her.

I pull back, my breath coming in ragged gasps as I look at her, my eyes locking onto hers. In that moment, the only thing that exists is her, and the way she makes me feel. It's as if we're in our own little bubble, a world that's separate from everything and everyone else.

She starts moving back and forth faster. Her hips grinding against mine, her hands roaming over my chest, my back, my neck. Her nails continue digging deeper into my skin. Leaving faint marks that only fuel my desire for her even more.

She pulls down my pants only enough to reveal my throbbing cock. Then she straddles me again, grinding her wet pussy against it. The sensation of her warm, slippery folds sliding against me is almost too much to bear. I can feel my desire for her growing with each movement.

Her moans grow louder. Her body writhes against mine in a rhythm that speaks of a passion that cannot be contained. I can feel her desire for my cock, urging me to fuck her right then and there.

But I want to prolong this pleasure, to savor every moment of our shared heat and passion. I know that I'll give her what she wants, but not yet, not until she's begging for it.

As I pull her close, I can feel the heat building between us. Her body is soft and warm against mine, and I'm filled with a deep need to fuck her.

I lift her up and place her on the kitchen counter, my lips finding hers in a fiery kiss. At the same time, I tease her entrance with the tip of my finger, knowing that only this small touch is driving her wild.

Then I lean down and drag my tongue slowly through her pussy. I apply just enough pressure to make her yelp in desperate pleasure. I want to fuck her brains out, but I also want to revel in this moment and let the intensity build between us.

As I slide my tongue a little deeper inside her, I can feel her body tense with desire. Her eyes roll back, and I know she would come right now if I were to flick my tongue against her clit.

But I don't want to rush this. I want to feel every part of her, to enjoy the moment, to explore every nook and cranny of her body. So, I pull back a little, teasing her again with the tip of my tongue, feeling her juices dripping into my mouth.

I can feel her body arching back, her hands pulling my head into her pussy, urging me on. When she finally begs, "Please, fuck me Ethan," I can't help but grin. I tease her entrance a bit more, flicking her clit lightly as she keeps moving her hips towards me, wanting it all.

Her hands still pushing my face closer and wanting more. I grab her arm and hold it down, whispering, "Patience." With another flick of my tongue, I press her clit harder and she moans so loud it sends shivers down my spine. I keep licking and sucking, licking and sucking, feeling her body tense with every motion.

I slip my fingers inside her, curling them in a hook-like motion. My other hand jerks off my cock, throbbing in anticipation of being inside her. She moves her hips towards me, her moans growing louder, and I know she's close. The way she writhes, her body trembling with pleasure, is an intoxicating sight.

Her body trembles as she whispers, "Y-yes, that's it. Fuck." I take in the taste of her, the scent of her arousal filling my senses. I don't change the rhythm of my fingers, teasing her with a relentless pleasure that drives her wild.

She continues her writhing motion, her legs shaking with pleasure. I can feel her desire for me, begging me to give her more. And I'm more than happy to oblige, my fingers finger-fucking her hard and deep.

I watch as her head goes back, her moans filling the air. I can feel her walls contracting around my fingers. Her orgasm builds to a crescendo that threatens to swallow her whole. And then she comes, her body convulsing on the counter, her juices flowing freely.

It's a mind-altering sight, one that leaves me breathless and wanting more. I continue to finger-fuck her, my movements slow and deliberate. Every moment of our shared passion is engrained in my memory.

As her body slowly comes down from the high of her orgasm, I pull back, my fingers glistening with her juices. I bring them up to my mouth, enjoying the taste of her, the smell of her juices still filling my senses. She watches me, her eyes heavy with desire, and I know that we're not done yet.

I help her off the counter as she wraps her legs around my waist, grabbing my neck to pull her lips to mine. Then she slides her legs down to the floor and then onto her knees. My heart races with anticipation.

Her small mouth takes in my big cock, and I can feel myself getting harder with each passing moment. I grunt aloud, my hands holding her head gently, not pushing, only guiding her rhythm. It's perfect, and I can feel myself getting lost in the pleasure of it all.

She sucks on my cock with such skill, taking me deep into her mouth, gagging a little, but never once stopping. The sensation is so slippery, with her spit coating my cock, making it feel like it's reaching her throat. I can't help but push her head deeper, harder, just enough to make her gag even more on my throbbing cock.

And then I come, my cock exploding in her mouth, filling her with my hot, sticky cum. She keeps sucking, swallowing every drop. Never once breaking eye contact with me, her gaze is filled with a lust and desire that leaves me breathless.

After I come in her mouth, she pulls back, a trail of saliva connecting my cock to her lips. And then she stands up, her lips finding mine in a fiery kiss. We kiss for what feels like hours, our shared passion and desire fueling every moment.

Eventually, we break apart, both of us realizing that we're exhausted, in need of sleep. I lift her into another deep kiss, her legs wrapping around my waist. We make our way to my bedroom, our bodies still entwined, and we fall asleep in each other's arms.

The heat of the moment has passed, but the passion and desire we shared are still as strong as ever. As we lie there, I know that we've only scratched the surface of what's possible between us.

There's so much more waiting for us in the days and weeks to come. I can't wait to explore every inch of her body, to savor every moment of our shared passion and desire.

13

THE GREEN-EYED MONSTER

ELLA

There's a tranquility to Ethan when he's asleep. He's all soft edges, his stern demeanor dissolving into the gentle rhythm of his breath. His chest rises and falls with a cadence that pulls me deeper into our shared warmth. His steady heartbeat hums like a lullaby against my cheek.

The sudden creak of the door breaks the quiet serenity. A soft, small voice echoes through the stillness. "Ella! You sleep here now?"

I turn to see Ollie standing by the door. His curly hair is in disarray and Mr. William, his favorite teddy bear is clutched firmly in his grasp. A wide smile breaks across my face. "Yes, sweetie, Ella slept here last night."

His big eyes blink up at me, the corners of his mouth curling up into an excited smile. "I'm hungry, Ella." His voice is earnest, the honesty of his simple declaration warming my heart.

Gently, I disentangle myself from Ethan. The cool morning air raises goosebumps on my skin. "What do you want to eat, little bird? Pancakes or eggs?"

He ponders this for a moment or two, his small brow furrowed as he holds Mr. William tighter. After a moment, his face brightens. "Hmm... Pancakes!"

Then a sleepy voice joins the conversation. "Good morning, Ella... morning, Ollie..." Ethan's words are drawled out, heavy with sleep. He sits up, rubbing his eyes before flashing a soft smile towards our enthusiastic little boy.

Ollie's excitement infects his father immediately. "Dad, wake up, we are having pancakes!"

Ethan chuckles, a deep, heartwarming sound. He looks towards me, his eyes filled with warmth. "Hey, Ella, can you make some pancakes for Mr. William too?" He playfully points towards the teddy bear in Ollie's arms.

Laughing, I nod. "Of course! Go to the kitchen and put on your apron. I'll be right there, champ!"

As Ollie happily skips out of the room, the door closes behind him, leaving Ethan and me alone once more. The quiet intimacy of the moment wraps around us like a warm blanket.

I settle back down beside Ethan, my head resting against his chest, his arm wrapping around me to pull me close. Our lips meet in a soft, lingering kiss, our breath mingling in the early morning air.

"Mmmm..." I hum into the kiss, my hands finding his, our fingers intertwining. In the soft glow of the morning light, our bodies entwined, this feels like the perfect start to the day.

The kitchen is bathed in the early morning sunlight. Everything is painted in warm golden hues. Ollie is already seated at the island.

His little legs swing excitedly as he watches me prepare the batter. The smell of vanilla and cinnamon fills the air, mingling with the sweet scent of maple syrup.

"Cinnamon pancakes, Ollie?" I ask, flipping the first pancake onto the hot griddle. He quickly claps his hands together. His laughter rings through the kitchen like the most joyful of melodies. "Yes, please!"

We chat about everything and nothing as I cook. Ollie regales me with tales of Mr. William's many adventures. His stories are filled with such innocence and creativity. It brings a comforting warmth to the room.

The clatter of a plate being set down next to Ollie interrupts his narration. Ethan joins us, a sleepy smile on his face as he playfully tousles Ollie's hair.

The pancakes are ready and served in no time, fluffy and golden, drenched in cinnamon and maple syrup. The three of us dig in, our conversation flowing around mouthfuls of food.

We discuss Ollie's adventures with Mr. William, and Ethan's recent work challenges. Sharing quiet smiles across the table and starting the day on a harmonious note.

As breakfast draws to a close, Ethan checks his watch. "Ollie, time to get ready for preschool, buddy."

Ollie grumbles but obediently slides off his chair. He runs off to get dressed and grab his backpack. Ethan turns to me, a thoughtful look in his eyes. "I can drop you off at class if you want, Ella."

My heart swells at his consideration. A part of me had been dreading the journey to class, but Ethan's offer brings relief. "Yeah, that would be great. Thank you, Ethan."

He nods, the corner of his mouth lifting in a small smile. "It's a pleasure."

A flurry of activity follows as we clean up the breakfast dishes. Ollie packs his backpack and I gather my own study materials. Soon, we're ready to leave.

The three of us, a trio that has become a family unit in such a short time, leaving together to face the world. As the garage door closes behind us, there is a sense of contentment. This is home.

ELLA

Mr. Sinclair begins his lecture on post-modern poetry and the obscurity of its symbols. I find my mind drifting away from the drone of his voice. The classroom fades into the background as a softer, warmer scene takes its place.

Ethan. His tousled hair in the morning light. The sleepy smile he graces me with before his first coffee. The deep timbre of his laughter echoing in my ears. A blush creeps up on my face as I remember the soft kisses we exchanged this morning. The intimacy of the moment still lingers in my senses.

My daydreaming is interrupted by a sharp poke in my ribs. As I snap back to reality, I find myself staring into the teasing eyes of Stacey, my classmate and best friend.

"Ugh, let me sleep," I groan, rubbing the sleep from my eyes.

Stacey smirks, leaning in closer. "Ethan not letting you sleep, huh?" she teases, her eyebrow raised suggestively.

"Oh, shut up, Stacey," I retort, my face flushing even more.

Stacey's smirk widens, a sparkle of curiosity lighting up her eyes. "Come on, tell me. Was it any good?"

I groan, covering my blushing face with my hands. "We didn't do anything for Christ's sake," I stammer out, my voice only a whisper. "Other than..."

Stacey leans closer, anticipation written all over her face. "Other than what?" she prods.

But before I could even utter another word, a stern voice interrupts us. "Ella, that's enough disruption. And see me after class."

The room turns deathly quiet. I lift my gaze from my desk and find myself locking eyes with Mr. Sinclair. Tall, broad-shouldered, with striking blue eyes and a perfect mess of sandy blonde hair.

He is a picture of rugged handsomeness. But his attractiveness doesn't help the situation. It only adds to the deep sense of embarrassment that's flooding me right now.

When the lecture ends, the other students file out as I gather my things slowly. I wait for my reprimand from Mr. Sinclair. Stacey winks with a teasing smirk to follow her as she struts out of the classroom. I roll my eyes at her as she exits, leaving me alone with him.

I settle back in my seat, nervously fiddling with the hem of my skirt. After a few minutes of tidying his papers and organizing his desk, Mr. Sinclair turns his attention to me. The classroom, devoid of its usual chatter, feels extra quiet under his stern gaze.

"Ella," he starts, his voice firm yet concerned. He steps away from his desk, his tall frame approaching my desk. The sudden closeness makes me tilt my head up to look at him, my heart pounding in my chest. "Is everything okay at home?"

"Yes...yeah," I manage to stutter, my fingers knotting into my skirt. He closes in on my desk, and his concern makes me uneasy.

He studies me for a moment, his piercing blue eyes softening a bit. "If anything is wrong, you can always tell me. As your teacher, I'm here to help."

His words linger in the air between us, the ambiguity of his statement causing alarms within me. But as I open my mouth to respond, the classroom door swings open.

Ethan steps in, his tall figure filling the doorway. His eyes dart between Mr. Sinclair and me. He has a hint of confusion, even a flicker of jealousy, invading his face.

"Mr. Sinclair," Ethan greets, his voice steady but I can detect a note of protective sternness in his tone. His gaze lingers on Mr. Sinclair for a moment before shifting to me, a silent question in his eyes.

"Professor Hartley," Mr. Sinclair nods in acknowledgment. He hastily pushes off my desk extends a hand towards Ethan. "I was about to finish up with Ella here."

Ethan's gaze never leaves me as he shakes Mr. Sinclair's hand. The atmosphere in the room changes subtly, the air growing heavy with an unspoken tension.

But then, with a final glance and a nod, Mr. Sinclair grabs his briefcase and steps past Ethan. "If you'll excuse me, I'm late for a meeting" as he hurries out of the room, leaving us alone. The door closing behind him sounds unusually loud. The two of us remain in the echoing silence of the empty classroom.

14

THE B-BOMB

ETHAN

"What were you talking about with Mr. Sinclair behind closed doors?" My words sound harsher than I intend. The question bursts forth from an unfamiliar jealous churn in my gut.

Ella blinks up at me, her wide eyes shining in a way I could not read. "I left class and went to the ladies' room when I felt sick. He was only filling me in on the material and the new assignment I missed. He was concerned..."

Her words trail off, and she has a slight frown, biting her lip and looking down at her hands. Her words should provide relief, but the burning sensation of jealousy doesn't fade. I don't want her near him. I don't want her near anyone else. And I hate that I can't explain why.

"Are you feeling better now? What happened?"

"Ethan, I'm fine. I felt hot and clammy for a few minutes. I splashed some water on my face and I'm better. Really. Nothing to worry about. And nothing to be jealous of," she adds with what sounds like a bit of amusement.

I'm briefly stunned, my mind reeling as I realize she has read the jealousy in my gut. "Ella, I'm glad you're feeling better. I just..." I begin, my voice faltering. I'm unsure how to explain the turmoil of emotions within me.

"I don't want him anywhere near you," I admit, my voice raw with the intensity of my feelings. "He has a reputation for getting involved with his female students."

She stays silent, the corners of her mouth tugging upwards in a small, understanding smile. "I'm not interested in Mr. Sinclair," she bluntly replies. "There's only one man I'm interested in."

Her admission sends a jolt through me, a flood of warmth spreading through my chest. I pull her closer, my hands instinctively resting on her waist. "Who might that be?" I murmur, leaning down so our faces are mere inches apart.

"Well," she whispers, her breath hitching as our noses brush. "He's standing right in front of me."

Her confession fills the space between us, a silent promise hanging in the air. The rest of the world fades into a blur. In that moment, all that matters is the two of us and the feelings that are impossible to ignore.

I draw in a sharp breath at her teasing look, my pulse thrumming in my ears. I don't know what game she's playing, but I'm willing to play it. My grip around her waist tightens, pulling her closer. There's no space for anything but the electric tension between us.

Her smile transforms into a gasp as our bodies meet. I bend down to her, my fingers finding their way to her neck. I exert a gentle pressure that makes her eyes flutter shut. The simple act sends a thrilling jolt through me, fueling my desire.

"God, Ethan," she moans softly, her voice a sultry whisper that reverberates down my spine. The sound of her saying my name, her voice laced with want, is pure intoxication.

Encouraged, I slowly lean in, brushing my lips lightly against hers. It's a soft kiss, tender and cautious, a taste of what's to come. Ella sighs into my mouth, her fingers reaching up to tangle in my hair.

The kiss deepens, our lips moving in a rhythm that's as natural as breathing. I pull her even closer, my hand sliding from her neck to rest at the small of her back, pressing her into me.

Ella's arms wrap around my neck, pulling me down to her. The pressure of her body against mine, the taste of her lips, the sound of her soft moans... it's all I could ever want.

She tastes like sunshine and secrets. A tantalizing mix that's as intoxicating as the finest wine. I can't get enough of her. The sweet scent of her skin, the warmth of her body against mine, the intoxicating way she makes me feel.

Our bodies move in perfect harmony, each touch, each kiss stoking the flame of our shared desire. It's a dance we're both familiar with, a dance that tells of a longing that can no longer be denied. And as I taste her, feel her, I realize that this... this is where I want to be. With her.

Still dazed from the passionate exchange, we simultaneously pull away. Breathless, our hearts pound in our chests. Ella's lips are swollen, her cheeks flushed to a lovely shade of pink. Her eyes still half-lidded with desire.

"Uhm," I stutter, feeling an unexpected sense of shyness creep in, "we ought to go." I finish my sentence awkwardly, the air thick with the electricity that has yet to dissipate.

She nods, flashing me a dazzling smile before quickly composing herself. "Yeah, we should."

The drive to Ollie's preschool is quiet. The atmosphere still buzzes with residual tension. But it's a comfortable silence, one filled with promise and shared understanding.

When my phone vibrates, I glance to read the text from my sister Alice.

> Don't you ever answer
> your phone, brother?
> I'm coming out to
> your house this evening.
> I have a surprise for you.

Alice. Surprise? Probably a suggestion or idea or set of plans for me and Ollie. I smile, remembering how well her idea about Ella worked out for us. The surprise might be on Alice this time!

When we arrive, the excitement in the air is unmistakable as the kids rush out of the building. Their chatter and laughter fill the air. I spot Ollie among the crowd, his bright smile standing out from the rest. My heart swells with joy as he runs towards our car.

"Ellaaaa!" he shouts, his joyous voice clear and crisp. As I open the back door, he dashes towards us. His small arms reaching out to hug Ella who's sitting in the back seat, his eyes alight with delight.

The way he clings to her, the love shining in his eyes. It's endearing. It's a sight that softens my heart and deepens my affection for both of them. Ella wraps her arms around him, her laughter ringing in the air. She showers him with affection, her hand ruffles his hair affectionately.

"Hey, Mr. Pancake Connoisseur!" she coos, a teasing lilt to her voice, "Did you have a good day at school?"

Ollie eagerly nods, his smile stretching from ear to ear. His eyes sparkle with excitement as he starts narrating his adventures of the day. I drive us back home, their laughter and chatter filling the car. The atmosphere is lively and heartwarming.

"Your Aunt Alice is coming to visit later, Ollie," I announce, for Ella's benefit more than Ollie's. My son barely acknowledges my statement, but Ella and I exchange glances and smiles.

As we pull into the driveway, Ollie is a bundle of energy in the back seat. Struggling to contain his excitement, he eagerly unlatches his seatbelt. He clambers out of the car, and the smile on Ella's face as she watches him is radiant. A reflection of the joy that Ollie exudes.

Once inside, the house fills with the comforting sounds of life. The clatter of shoes being kicked off. The murmur of voices and laughter echoing through the rooms. The familiar hum of appliances in the background.

Ella leads the charge into the kitchen, rolling up her sleeves with a determined grin. Ollie asks for pancakes for dinner. We can't really complain. "Alright, Mr. Pancake," she teases. Her eyes twinkle with amusement as she tousles Ollie's hair. "Are you ready to be Chef Ollie?"

Ollie's laughter fills the room as he scrambles onto a stool, his head nodding in agreement. His joy is infectious, spreading to Ella and me as we gather around the kitchen island. We're ready to begin our culinary adventure.

Ella, always prepared, starts to pull out ingredients and utensils from the cupboards. There are bowls, a whisk, a measuring cup, and various ingredients. She lines them up on the counter, narrating the steps to Ollie who is hanging on her every word.

"Should I set a plate for Aunt Alice?" Ella inquires. I shrug in reply.

I continue to watch the two of them, the scene before me warming my heart. The sight of Ella, vibrant and beautiful.

She shows Ollie how to measure the flour, and how to crack an egg without getting shell in the bowl. And how to whisk the ingredients together without making a mess is a tough one for him.

The scent of cooking pancakes fills the kitchen as Ella skillfully flips them. She makes it look so easy, her slender fingers guiding the spatula with practiced ease. She has an effortless grace about her, a rhythm and fluidity in her movements. It's hypnotizing to watch her skirt flow freely with each move of her hips.

Ollie, ever the eager learner, watches in rapt attention. He tries to mimic her movements. His tiny hands grasp the spatula, his brow furrowed in concentration. It's a beautiful sight, one that tugs at my heartstrings.

After a while, I join them, adding my own touches to the pancakes. I spread some butter on them while they're still hot, then sprinkle them with cinnamon sugar. It's a small task, but it feels meaningful, being a part of this moment, contributing to our shared activity.

Finally, when the pancakes are cooked to a perfect golden brown, we sit down together at the dinette table. The delicious aroma fills the air. Ollie can't help but let out a delighted squeal, his little hands reaching for the tempting stack.

It's a perfect evening, filled with laughter and love. As I look around at the two people who mean the world to me, I can't help but feel a profound sense of gratitude. It's been a long journey filled with many trials and tribulations. But in this moment, with Ella and Ollie by my side, I am the luckiest man alive.

Then the doorbell rings.

"Sounds like Aunt Alice is here," I say as I move to answer the bell. Ella gives me a glance, but Ollie is too involved in his story to pay attention.

I am smiling broadly as I pull open the door without hesitation. But the door frames a stranger rather than my sister.

He stands there in the fading daylight. His silhouette is outlined by the soft, golden hues of the setting sun.

He looks young, with short, dark hair that's a little ruffled, as if he just rolled out of bed. His arms are adorned with intricate tattoos in a kaleidoscope of colors. The designs contrast sharply against the black T-shirt he's wearing.

"Hey," he says, his voice low and raspy. His eyes, dark and piercing, meet mine, giving off an air of defiance.

"Hi," I reply cautiously, squinting a little to get a better look at him. "Can I help you?"

His eyes dart past me, scanning the interior of the house. "I heard Ella lives here. Ella Parker. Can I talk to her?" he asks, a hint of impatience creeping into his voice.

My mind races, trying to make sense of his words. "Who are you?" I find myself asking before I can stop myself.

His gaze snaps back to me, a dark glint in his eyes. "Why do you care and who the fuck are you?" he shoots back, his tone sharp. He takes a step forward, his body language screaming aggression. But I refuse to be intimidated, I know I can handle myself if it comes to that.

"Wow, step back," I reply, raising my hands in a placating gesture. His audacity astounds me. I was not expecting this.

And then he drops the bombshell.

"I am her boyfriend, now move outta the way."

The world screeches to a halt. Boyfriend? What? The word reverberates in my mind, causing my heart to pound in my chest.

Before I can respond, Ella appears from the living room. Her eyes widen as she spots the man standing on our doorstep. "Matt?" she gasps, the color draining from her face. I can see the shock on her face, mirroring my own.

"Hi my love. Have you missed me?" He flashes her a smug grin, ignoring my presence completely.

My heart drops to the pit of my stomach. The implications of his words are sinking in and it feels like I've been punched in the gut.

15

A Surprise from the Past

ELLA

A cold wave of dread cascades through me as Matt's words echo in the hushed silence of Ethan's home. A place that has become a sanctuary, my sanctuary, now tainted by the invasion of an unwelcome past.

Boyfriend? The word sits heavily in the air, a thundercloud ready to burst. The tension is almost a tangible entity searing through the air. I can feel Ethan's muscles coil next to me in defensive stance.

"Matt," I manage to force out his name, the single syllable tasting like rusted metal on my tongue. "You're not my boyfriend." My voice, usually so full of life and cheer, now feels like a frail shadow of itself. It trembles with a concoction of fear, anger, and disbelief.

Panic surges into the pit of my stomach, the taste of fear and disgust stinging my mouth as my body begins to shake. "Please leave. You don't belong here. You have no right to intrude."

His eyes narrow, his gaze zeroing in on me, as if trying to dissect my thoughts. "So, you're saying I've traveled all the way out here for nothing?"

He scoffs, his eyes sweeping over the spacious living room and the perfect décor. "Nice place you've got here, Ella. What are you doing now, slutting yourself out so you can have a place to sleep?"

His words hit me like a blow, raw and painful, and I'm momentarily speechless. As the full weight of his accusations seep in, my heart hammers in my chest.

My mind whirls with disbelief and anger twisting into a dangerous knot in my stomach. My skin flushes, a mixture of mortification and rage simmering beneath the surface.

I'm about to defend myself against his vile accusations when a fist shoots out of nowhere. Ethan. It happens fast. One second Matt's standing there, smirking, and the next he's reeling backward. His hand clutches his bloodied mouth.

Ethan's knuckles are red, but his face is an impassive mask of fury. The silence that follows is deafening. A stark contrast to the fiery sparks of anger dancing in Ethan's eyes, the world seems to hold its breath.

Matt stumbles back, cradling his face. His vicious smirk replaced with an expression of pure shock. The satisfaction that washes over me is a dark, bitter taste, but it's a balm to the hurt his words had left.

Heat rises in my chest, a tempest of emotions swirling within me as I watch Ethan's taut profile. His voice resonates in the still room, a low growl that leaves no room for dispute. "Don't ever come back here, you hear me?"

Instead of stepping back, Matt's face contorts into a snarl, and he launches himself at Ethan. I let out a startled gasp, my hands wringing together in a futile attempt to calm my rapid heart. Their bodies crash together, a tangled mess of clenched fists and gritted teeth.

The harsh slap of skin against skin echoes around us as Ethan expertly dodges Matt's punches. Ethan throws a few well-aimed hits of his own. His body moves like liquid, each blow executed with precision.

He's a man who knows how to defend himself, and those he cares for. I watch in awe, and more than a little fear. The man I've come to know as gentle, patient Ethan transforms into a protective, fierce being.

"Ethan, stop!" I find myself shouting, my voice barely heard over the grunts and scuffling sounds. I can see the danger in his movements. He's driven by a blend of fury and protectiveness. It's a dangerous combination that threatens to spiral out of control.

My plea slices through the heavy tension, bringing Ethan to a halt. His chest heaves as he steps back from Matt, his gaze still locked on the other man. Blood stains Matt's lips and he spits a globule of it on the floor, his face a rictus of pain and humiliation.

"Get out of this house, off my property, and don't come back," Ethan hisses.

"This isn't over yet," Matt spits out, his voice carrying the sting of a threat, his eyes narrowed to slits.

The heavy front door slams shut behind him, his departing words lingering in the room. An ominous shadow is cast over my safe place. The only sound remaining is the labored breathing of Ethan and my own racing heartbeat.

"Ethan... are you okay?" I whisper, my voice trembling as I move towards him. His body is rigid, muscles taut as if bracing for another attack. But his gaze softens as he meets my eyes.

"Yeah. Yeah, I'm fine," he replies, his voice hoarse from the adrenaline. His eyes cloud with worry, his gaze roaming over me, searching for any sign of distress. "How could he... find us?" His words hang in the air like an icy potion, sending a chill through me.

"I... I don't know," I admit, my voice only a whisper. The thought of Matt stalking me, finding his way to this sanctuary, sends a wave of dread crashing over me. "He might have stalked me or something... I don't... I don't know..." My voice breaks, a sob catching in my throat.

Hot tears spill from my eyes, leaving a burning trail down my cheeks. My vision blurs as the reality of the situation crashes down around me. There's a surge of vulnerability, a fear I haven't felt since I met Ethan.

I'm dizzy, wobbling from the scene that happened right before my eyes. My gentle Ethan brought down to this low level by my biggest nightmare. My vision is clouded by the image of my life with Ethan and Oliver collapsing like a house of cards.

Ethan's warm hands cups my face, his thumbs gently wiping away my tears. "Shhh... it's okay, baby girl. You're safe here. Safe with me." His voice soothes my frazzled nerves, his words a promise he intends to keep.

As his lips find mine in a tender kiss, my heart's frantic rhythm begins to slow, each beat syncing with his. His taste, the strong firmness of his body against mine, grounds me, tethering me to the moment.

The world outside, with all its chaos, fades into insignificance as I lose myself in the calm of his embrace.

My heart clenches at the sight of Ollie huddled behind the couch, his wide eyes shining with terror. "Ollie..." I call in a whispered voice, opening my arms to him. His frightened gaze shifts between me and Ethan, his little body trembling.

"It's okay," I assure him, my voice now above a whisper. "Everything is okay." My tone is steady, but inside, my heart aches for him, for the fear he must have felt. For the fact that his safe haven was threatened, even if only for a moment.

Carefully, he emerges from his hiding spot. His small body dwarfs in comparison to the living room around him. His gaze is cautious as he inches towards us, his small hands fisted in the hem of his shirt.

As he steps into my open arms, I gather him close, his tiny body pressed squeezed between Ethan and me. His arms wrap around my neck, and Ethan's hand smooths reassuring circles onto his back.

As Ollie's sobs subside, we hold him, offering him the protection and comfort he needs. For the moment, I am safe. I feel complete.

The doorbell interrupts the moment and the three of us tense. Ethan disengages from our embrace to open the door. Ollie and I hold each other and listen. Ethan's greeting to Alice is a relief to both of us.

"Hi, Sis, come in," Ethan's voice is steady, then joined by Alice and another voice exchanging greetings. When Ethan returns, he is followed by Alice as well as a slender brunette beauty with her arm circling his waist.Su

Alice takes charge of the situation. She greets Ollie and me in a friendly way, then introducing the brunette.

"Lydia, this is Oliver and his nanny, Ella. This is Lydia Swanson, an old friend of the family, who went to high school with Ethan."

Alice doesn't say sweetheart or girlfriend, but that is what I hear, what I know from the way Lydia is looking at Ethan. Ethan's face is hard to read, but his cheeks are flushed and his eyes are staring hard at me.

I recognize the jealousy flooding my body. I caution myself once again to keep control of my emotions, my voice, my expression. I will be strong; I will follow Ethan's lead. I will be the nanny and not the lover. I am the nanny, my mind repeats.

As Alice explains that Lydia came to her studio today, I try to avoid Ethan's eyes as I continue to hold Ollie close. Ethan leaves the room and I take the opportunity to explain that I was just about to put Ollie to bed.

"Tell Aunt Alice and her friend good night, Sweetie." Ollie goes to each of the women and gives them each a reluctant hug. When Ethan returns with a bottle of wine and four glasses, he hugs Oliver and tells him he will look in on him later.

"And I have some homework to finish, so I guess it's good night for me too," I explain. "Happy to meet you Lydia, and good to see you again, Alice."

Ethan's eyes follow me as Ollie and I leave the room, but his words are for his sister and her companion. Guiding Ollie back to his room, I settle him into bed. It's a comforting routine that brings a semblance of normalcy back into our evening.

His eyelids flutter closed, his breaths even out as sleep takes him away from the worries of the world. I tuck him in gently, pressing a kiss to his forehead before slipping out of the room. I leave the door slightly ajar in case he calls for me.

The sounds of light laughter and conversation drift to me as I pause in the hallway. I go into my guest bedroom and collapse on the bed, fully clothed. In a matter of seconds, full body sobs overtake me. I am lost under the weight of a mixture of emotions deep and unidentifiable.

16

IMPOSSIBLE TO RESIST

ELLA

The glow of the bedside clock reads 2:47 as I peer through small slits of my tear swollen eyes. I roll onto my back listening for sounds in the house.

I tiptoe into Ollie's room and see that he is lost in the easy sleep of the young. I turn toward the family room and creep down the hallway, uncertain of what I would find. Fearful of facing Ethan, but more fearful of not knowing where things stood between us.

Ethan is standing at the window, looking into the moonlit garden. I approach him silently, my steps barely making a sound against the wooden floor. His back is to me, the lines of his muscular form visible through the thin fabric of his shirt.

"Ethan..." I begin, my voice a whisper, not wanting to shatter the quiet that has fallen over us. Without another word, I wrap my arms around him from behind. I press myself into the broad expanse of his back. His body stiffens at first, but then relaxes, his hand coming up to cover one of mine.

"I'm so sorry," I murmur against his back, my words muffled by his shirt. He doesn't reply, but his grip on my hand tightens, a silent acknowledgment of my words. We stand there, wrapped in our thoughts and the protective hold of each other. We find solace in the silence that envelops us.

The sound of his voice, low and soothing, sends a wave of relief washing over me. He turns to face me, his hands on my shoulders. "Don't be sorry, Ella. None of this is your fault."

His hand gently tilts my head up so our eyes meet. His gaze holds a warmth that softens the harsh lines of his face. The hint of a promise in his eyes that is a comfort to my distressed soul.

He leans down and presses a chaste kiss on my forehead. His lips linger for a moment longer than necessary. It's a small act, but one that sends my heart into flutters.

I look up at him, caught in the earnest intensity of his gaze. He's so close that the soft glow from the room's ambient lighting gives him a celestial glow.

Without breaking our gaze, he steps back. His hands slide down my back from my shoulders to my waist, pulling me flush against him.

There's an unspoken question in his eyes as he leans down, his lips mere inches from mine. I can feel the heat radiating from him, a magnetic pull that's impossible to resist. I close my eyes, leaning in to close the distance between us.

When our lips finally meet, it's soft and gentle. A stark contrast to the intensity of the emotions coursing through us. His kiss is careful, almost reverential, as if he's afraid to scare me away. But the gentleness doesn't last.

As he deepens the kiss, a surge of passion takes over, washing away all traces of restraint.

His hands roam freely over my body, leaving a trail of heated skin in their wake. The world outside ceases to exist as we get lost in the moment. The breathtaking intimacy is binding us together.

Ethan's lips travel from mine down to my neck, his warm breath against my skin sending shivers down my spine. I let my fingers explore the firm muscles of his back, reveling in the primal groan that escapes his lips.

He lifts me up, and I wrap my legs around his waist. Our lips never part, as if the kiss could last forever. I feel his strength as he carries me to the bedroom.

17

Affirmation

ELLA

The anticipation builds up inside me, and my heart races as he throws me on the bed. He stands over me and skillfully slides my skirt and panties off and to the floor in one quick move. Then he lifts my shirt off over my head revealing my bare breasts. He gets on top of me, holding my arms above my head with one of his strong hands.

The intensity of his gaze is like a flame that ignites a fire within me. His eyes are burning with desire, and I can't help but get goosebumps all over me. I am completely at his mercy, and the thought sends a rush of excitement through my veins.

As he leans down, his lips graze my ear, and his hot breath sends waves of pleasure through my body. With a husky voice, he whispers, "You're mine. And nobody can take you away from me."

His words set me ablaze, and I can feel the blood rushing down to my crotch. As my body surrenders to the heat of the moment, I bite my lip, consumed by the intensity of his desire.

I can feel the raw passion radiating from him, as he presses his body against mine, pinning me down with his weight. His lips are on my neck, and I can feel the heat emanating from him. He kisses me hungrily, as if he can't get enough of me.

I let out a soft moan, and he pulls back, his eyes searching mine for permission. I nod, and he takes that as a cue to continue. He kisses me again, and this time it's more intense, more passionate.

His hands roam over my body, and I gasp as he finds the sensitive spots. His touch is electric, and I can't help but arch my back, wanting more.

He breaks the kiss, and there's a sudden pang of loss, until his lips find mine again. He kisses me hard, his tongue exploring my mouth. His big hard cock is against my thigh, and I know that it's aching to be inside me.

He breaks away to stand and look down at my naked body with an insatiable lust. Oh, I want him to fuck me so bad. It's been weeks since I've craved his touch like this.

Watching him take his shirt off only intensifies the need inside me. His muscles and chest are a sight to behold, and I can't look away from his intense stare.

Our eyes locked, he slides his pants and boxers down to the floor. His delectable dick ready to fuck me.

He pushes forward and takes my arms above my head again. My anticipation is almost unbearable as I feel his other hand between my legs, his fingers inside me, filling me up completely. It's a sensation that makes me clench around him, wanting more. Slowly and carefully, he presses his thumb against my clit, sending waves of pleasure through me.

I can't help but beg for him, my breathless pleas and curses falling from my lips. "Ethan, please," I moan, completely at his mercy. The raw passion between us is like nothing else, and I surrender to the heat of the moment. I'm consumed by the intensity of his desire.

"Please what?" he teases, "What do you want, my pretty?" He dominates me completely, his hand and thumb bringing me to the brink of ecstasy over and over again. I am his, completely, and I can't imagine being anywhere else but in his grasp.

"What do you want, pretty?" he repeats, his voice laced with dominance. "Beg for it."

I shudder at the sound of his commanding voice, feeling the power he holds over me. "Please, Ethan," I gasp, my breath itching with need. "I need you inside me. I need you to fuck me hard and make me yours."

"Look at me." It was a growl deep from his chest and fuck if that didn't make my cunt throb even more.

He knows what I want, and he's going to give it to me - on his terms. He smirks, his eyes narrowing as he takes in the sight of me, spread out and ready for him.

"You want me, don't you?" he growls, the sound sending a shiver down my spine. "You want me to take you and make you mine."

I nod, unable to speak as he positions himself at my entrance. He's going to fuck me raw, and I'm going to love every second of it. The thought alone is enough to make me moan, my body arching up to meet his.

He doesn't give me a chance to catch my breath before he's slamming into me. His thickness consumes me completely. I gasp, my arms now freed, my hands clawing at his back. He takes me hard and fast. The pain quickly gives way to pleasure, and I can feel myself getting wetter and wetter with every thrust.

He's not gentle, not by a long shot. He's rough, primal, taking what he wants from me without mercy. But it's exactly what I need, what I crave - to be dominated, to be taken completely.

As he speeds up, his hands move to my shoulders, pinning me down with his weight. I can feel his breath hot against my ear, his lips grazing my skin as he whispers in a low, menacing growl.

"You're mine," he says, his voice laced with possession.

I nod, too lost in the pleasure and heat of the moment to form words. I'm completely at his mercy, and I wouldn't want it any other way. With every thrust, every moan, every gasp, I'm his. Completely and wholly consumed by the intensity of our desire.

He flips me over with force, making it feel like I'm but a toy for him to play with. I'm on my stomach, my back arched lifting my ass up high, and I spread my cheeks for him, inviting him in. He teases me, his cock head grazing my rear entrance, the expectation is driving me wild.

I try to grab him with my hands, but he holds them behind my back, denying me the pleasure I so desperately crave. "Fuck me already, Ethan!" I beg, my voice dripping with need and desire.

He doesn't waste any time. He thrusts into me hard and fast, his cock filling me up completely and stretching me to my limits. He fucks me with such intensity, pulling my hair and driving me wild with each and every stroke.

I can't get enough of it – and I'm loving every second of being completely dominated by him. "N-never felt anything l-like this before, fucking god, shit, fuck!" I cussed and this only made him fuck me harder.

He kept spanking my ass, leaving red marks that would last for days. Even though he was fucking me hard and fast, he made sure that I was enjoying every moment of it.

He knew - he knew that I was craving him more than anything, that I would do anything to feel his cock deep inside me. I screamed out his name, cursing and begging for more, my body consumed by the hot passion and desire between us.

"Come for me," he growls, his voice laced with raw desire.

The heat radiates from him, a magnetic pull that's impossible to resist. I scream his name, my muscles seize and the wave finally crashes, stars exploding behind my eyes as I come with a loud cry.

The aftershocks of my orgasm leave me pleasantly limp, and he whispers in my ear, "That's my good girl." But he doesn't stop, his cock growing harder and harder inside me.

With a final thrust, he comes deep inside me, emptying his load. It leaves me completely and fully consumed by the intensity of our desire.

Afterwards, he rolls us to our side, me spooned into him, his arms wrapped around me in a tight embrace. The intensity of the moment fades away, replaced by a warm sense of contentment. He strokes my hair, his fingers gentle against my scalp, as we both catch our breath.

"Are you okay?" he whispers in my ear, his voice soft and caring.

I nod, feeling safe and loved in his arms. "More than okay," I say, my voice barely a whisper.

He rolls me over to face him. He smiles, his eyes warm and affectionate. "Good," he says, his thumb tracing circles on my back. "I just wanted to make sure you're okay."

I snuggle closer to him, feeling the warmth of his body against mine. The passion and desire may have faded, but the intensity of our connection is stronger than ever. In his arms, I know I'm exactly where I'm meant to be - safe, loved, and cared for.

As we lay there, sated and content, I know that this is just the beginning of something amazing. A connection that goes beyond the physical, a love that's deeper than anything I've ever known. And with him by my side, I know that I'll never have to go through life alone again.

18

FALLING INTO PLACE

ETHAN

The morning greets me with a mélange of warm hues painting the sky. The sunshine announces the arrival of another promising day. I rub the sleep from my eyes, the tangle of bed sheets an evident remnant of last night's passion.

As I pull myself from the cocoon of warmth, my mind is flooded with memories of our lovemaking. The way her lips felt against mine, the soft moans she had tried to stifle, her hands running up and down my back. It sends a jolt of electricity down my spine, a reminder of the spark that has kindled between us.

I slip on a pair of jeans and a loose t-shirt, my bare feet smack against the cool floor as I make my way towards the kitchen. The enticing aroma of freshly brewed coffee reaches me before I even round the corner. It's pulling me in like a moth to a flame.

There she is, the vision of perfection that Ella presents in my oversized t-shirt, her long legs bared for me to see. The sight of her is like a breath of fresh air, the first light of the dawn.

Her back is to me as she hums along to a tune playing softly from the radio, lost in the peaceful rhythm of the morning. Sneaking up, I wrap my arms around her waist from behind, pulling her against me. The contact makes her jump, the mixing spoon she's holding clatters against the bowl.

"Ethan!" she exclaims, her voice feigning annoyance. But the light giggle that follows betrays her true feelings.

I lean in, my lips grazing her ear as I murmur, "Good morning." A shiver runs through her at my words, a subtle reaction that doesn't go unnoticed by me. The sound of her laugh fills the room, a melodious sound that has become my favorite.

"Ethan, I can't focus like this," she teases, but she doesn't pull away. Instead, she leans back against me, her body molding into mine. I tighten my grip around her, relishing the feel of her in my arms.

The sight of her in my baggy t-shirt stirs a rush of desire that is undeniable. Yet I find myself content with the domesticity of the moment. It's a simple morning, yet one that holds a certain charm. A quiet peace that I hadn't realized I had been missing until Ella came into my life.

The breakfast preparation continues. Our movements synchronize as we work together in perfect tandem. The casual touches and the exchanged smiles envelop us in a shared bubble. The comfortable silence is a reminder of the bond that's been building between us.

We sit down to eat, Ollie joining us with a sleepy yawn and a rumbling stomach. As I look at Ella, her soft smile is directed towards Ollie as the serene morning light illuminates her.

I can't help but feel a sense of absolute contentment. It's as if everything I've ever wanted, everything I've ever needed, is right here in front of me.

I didn't know what to expect when Ella came into our lives, but this... This peace. This comfort. This burning desire and the affectionate intimacy is all more than I could have ever hoped for.

Feeling the vibration in my pocket, I pull out my phone to find Alice's name lighting up the screen. I sigh and take a deep breath. "Hey, Alice," I greet her, my tone betraying the surprise of her call.

"Hey, Ethan! I thought I'd call and check on my favorite big brother. How are things this morning? It was a surprise to see Lydia last night, wasn't it? I had a great time. I'm sure she would like to see you again. Don't you think it's time you started acting like a bachelor again? And a very attractive, eligible one, too." Her voice is warm and lighthearted, the same as always, and I can't help but smile.

"Yes, Lydia was quite the surprise last night." I lean back into my chair, glancing towards Ella, who's helping Ollie clean up the breakfast dishes.

"We didn't get a chance to get into it last night, Alice. But things are really great right now, with Ella here. Ollie is crazy about her. We are settling into a wonderful routine."

Alice's laugh filters through the phone, a sound that's become rare over the past few years. "Sounds boring," she teases, her words echoing the playful nature we've always shared.

"Aren't you missing the excitement of your bachelor life? Lydia is available and interested. Let me....."

Rolling my eyes at her assumption, I cut her off. "Hardly, Alice. My life is full of enough excitement with Ollie, I assure you."

I let out a low chuckle, running a hand through my hair as I contemplate how to answer. "Ella... she's been great. She's great with Ollie, and..." I trail off, the words catching in my throat.

"And?" Alice prompts, her tone suddenly intrigued. "What's that pause for, Ethan?"

"Well, um... We're..." I stammer, feeling an unexpected surge of nerves. It's silly. It's only Alice. I can talk to her about anything. But this feels different. Bigger.

"We're what?" Alice prods, her curiosity piqued. "Ethan, you're not leaving me in suspense, are you?"

"We're involved, we're dating." I finally confess as the words come tumbling out before I can second-guess them. I glance at Ella, to be sure she heard my declaration, and I receive a warm, mischievous grin in return.

Alice gasps with a dramatic pause, the sound echoing through the phone. "No way!" she exclaims, her voice pitched higher than I've heard in years. "You and Ella? As in, Ella Parker, Ollie's nanny? You're dating? I totally missed that last night. "

"Yeah, Alice," I confirm, chuckling at her theatrics. "Ella and me. We're... we're together."

"Oh my God!" Alice squeals, a sound so unexpected that I have to pull the phone away from my ear for a second. "This is the best news! I mean, who would have thought? You, my big, grumpy brother, dating again! And with Ella, of all people!"

Her words, although teasing, hold a note of sincerity. I know she means well, and that she's happy for me. But still, I can't help but feel a blush creeping up my neck at her enthusiastic reaction. "Alright, Alice, don't make a big deal out of it."

"Too late!" she laughs, her joy infectious. "This is big, Ethan! You'll have to tell me all about it when we meet up. But for now, don't think another thing about Lydia having her sights set on you. I'll nip that in the bud today! Well, I'll let you go. I just wanted to hear your voice. And now that I have this juicy bit of gossip, my day is complete."

With that, she hangs up, leaving me with a quiet chuckle and a warmth in my chest. My little sister, as cheeky as ever, but it's her support that makes this all the more special.

I join Ella and Ollie in the living room, back to the serenity of our morning. I realize, with a startling clarity, how everything is falling into place.

"Mail's here!" Ella's voice chimes through the house, sounding distractingly sweet as always.

I glance up from my spot on the couch, where Ollie and I are engaged in a fierce battle of toy cars. "Can you grab it, Elle?" I ask, absentmindedly steering a red race car along the edge of the coffee table.

She nods, her fingers sifting through the small pile of letters and envelopes. "Anything important?" I ask, my attention divided between our miniature Grand Prix and the soft sound of her sweet voice.

"No... umm, just the usual stuff, you know." Ella responds, her words wavering a little, unusual for her confident tone.

Her off-hand comment sparks a small alarm in my mind, but I push it aside. I focus instead on Ollie's excited giggles as he sends his toy car flying across the room. Ella puts the mail on the end table and joins us on the floor. Her expression is a little distant, and her movements are lacking their usual vivacity.

Our morning spirals into a flurry of laughter and play. A delicate web of happiness is woven from the simple joy of being together. And yet, there's an undercurrent of something different. Something unspoken that I can't quite put my finger on.

I catch Ella's eyes drifting to the stack of mail several times, mentally flipping through the envelopes before she quickly looks away. I could ask her about it. I could reach out, reassure her, remind her that we're in this together.

But something holds me back. My instinct says that she needs time to process whatever it is that's bothering her. If she wants to talk, she'll talk. And I'll be here, ready to listen, ready to offer whatever comfort or advice I can give.

So I don't ask. I don't push. I simply slide my hand over hers, giving it a gentle squeeze. A silent promise of support. A reminder that she's not alone. And from the soft smile she gives me in return, I know she understands.

I'm thinking back to her ex-boyfriend, the way he showed up unannounced, the way he tried to intimidate her. The thought makes my blood boil.

But then I look at Ella, strong and beautiful, her resilience shining brighter than ever. And I know that whatever this is, we can handle it. Together.

As our day slips into evening, Ella's mood doesn't improve, but she doesn't shut down either. She's present and engaging with both Ollie and me. She's laughing at our antics, even joining in when the mood strikes her. It's a subtle change in her demeanor, but it's there. Lurking in the background like a ghost, impossible to ignore.

But for now, we let it be. We carry on with our day, enjoying the simple pleasures of our shared space, our shared life. A quiet understanding passes between us. Whatever's going on, we'll face it, just as we've faced everything else. Together. As a team. As a family.

19

SILENT FAREWELL

ELLA

The day unravels like an old tapestry. Threads of joy and fear intertwining to form a scene that's both beautiful and haunting. Ethan is a calm and steady presence that anchors me amid the turbulent emotions that threaten to pull me under.

I can't tell him, though. I can't burden him with the storm raging inside me. It started so normally, with the delivery of the mail. Another stack of letters, bills and advertisements. But one letter stood out.

One envelope with no postage, only my name printed in large letters. One envelope screaming danger. One envelope that sent me to the guest room to open.

Matt.

The writing was familiar, each curve and flourish a vivid reminder of the past. I opened it without thinking. My mind only registered who it was from when I saw his crude handwriting staring back at me.

He was threatening me. He was threatening Ethan. He claimed he would ruin Ethan's career for sleeping with a student if I didn't leave Ethan's house and go back to him.

A bitter growl bubbles up from my throat, the irony not lost on me. He thinks I'm still his, that he still has some power over me. But I'm not that naive girl anymore. I refuse to be bullied by him.

But the threat to Ethan... that sends a fresh wave of terror crashing over me. I don't want Ethan to get hurt because of me. He doesn't deserve that. He deserves someone who won't bring danger and trouble into his life. He deserves someone who can give him peace, not chaos.

I clutch the letter tighter, the edge of the paper digging into my palm. I should tell Ethan. I should show him the letter, tell him what's happening. But the words won't come. How can I tell him that my past is threatening to ruin his future?

Throughout the day, I try to maintain a facade of normalcy. Participating in playtime with Ollie, preparing meals, doing mundane chores. But it's like I'm moving through a haze, my thoughts consumed by the letter and its implications.

Ethan, bless his heart, doesn't push. I can see the concern in his eyes, the questions he's holding back, but he gives me space. He seems to understand that I need time, that I'm wrestling with something I'm not yet ready to share.

I long to lean on him, to let him hold me and tell me that everything will be okay. But this isn't his battle to fight, it's mine. The last thing I want is to bring more trouble into his life, into our life. Because that's what it's become, hasn't it? *Our* life. And I'll be damned if I let Matt ruin that.

But for now, I say nothing. I keep my fears locked away, a silent torment gnawing at my heart. I know I can't keep this secret forever. Eventually, I will have to face it. But for now, I will hold onto the fragile peace we've carved out in our little corner of the world. I have to trust it won't shatter under the weight of my past.

The realization hits me like a freight train, the finality of it sinking in with every passing second. Leaving. That's the only way to protect Ethan, to shield him from the toxic fallout of my past.

The thought feels like a physical blow, leaving me breathless. This home, this family that Ethan and I have created is everything I've ever dreamed of. Everything I didn't even know I wanted. But it's the thought of losing him, of inflicting pain upon him that is too much to bear.

I look at Ethan as he plays with Ollie, their laughter filling the house with a warmth that tugs at my heartstrings. I watch as he lifts Ollie high into the air, the little boy's giggles echoing throughout the house.

My heart aches with a profound love for these two people who have become my world.

Tonight, I'll say goodbye. A silent farewell to the life I could have had, the life we could have built.

Tonight, I'll give myself to Ethan completely. I'll etch every detail, every sensation into my mind. I'll memorize the way he looks at me, the way his fingers feel against my skin, the warmth of his lips on mine.

A part of me wishes I could tell him, to explain why I'm leaving. But I know that would only make things harder. Ethan would insist on fighting, on protecting me. He wouldn't understand that by doing so, he'd be putting himself in harm's way.

Tonight, I will be Ella, the woman that Ethan loves, the woman that loves him with every fiber of her being. I will not be the woman running from her past, the woman whose secrets threaten to tear everything apart.

As I prepare for the night, I can't help but feel the weight of the decision I've made trying to drag me under. It sits heavy in my heart, a constant reminder of what I'm about to lose.

But this isn't about me anymore. It's about Ethan, about Ollie. They deserve a life filled with happiness, not one tainted by my past mistakes.

And so, I make a silent vow to myself. No matter how much it hurts, no matter how much my heart breaks, I will do what's best for them.

I will leave.

Even if it shatters me.

A palpable excitement fills the kitchen as I begin to cook our dinner. I've chosen to make Ethan's favorite dish. It's a simple Spaghetti Bolognese, the sauce simmering on the stove. It fills the house with a rich, tantalizing aroma.

A meal for a family, our family. The normalcy of it all stings, a bitter reminder of the decision I've made.

"Dinner smells good!" Ethan calls from the living room, the cheerful lilt in his voice causing an ache in my heart.

I respond with a forced smile, calling back, "Almost ready!"

His words carry a warmth that feels like life to my troubled soul. The simple pleasure of preparing a meal for those I love feels painfully precious.

I hear Ollie's excited chatter as he joins Ethan in the living room. Their joyous banter fills the house with a wonderful energy. It takes all my strength to stop the tears welling from up in my eyes.

As I serve the dinner, I try to memorize every moment, every detail. Ethan's approving nod as he takes his first bite. Ollie's cheerful chatter. The comforting sounds of our cutlery against the plates. The warmth of the room. Each detail, each moment feels immensely precious.

Throughout dinner, we laugh, we share stories, and we enjoy the meal. But beneath it all, a silent clock is ticking away in my heart, each tick echoing my impending departure.

After we finish eating, I help Ollie practice his numbers and enjoy the simplicity of the task. The innocent queries he poses, the way his eyes light up when he succeeds - these are the moments I'll miss the most. These are the memories I'll hold onto when I'm far away from here.

As the night draws to a close, I look at Ethan, the man who has shown me love in its purest form. My heart tightens in my chest as he smiles at me, unaware of the secret I'm harboring.

Tonight, we'll make love. Tonight, we'll share a connection deeper than any we've ever shared before. But with the dawn, I will be gone. And I can only hope that someday, he'll understand why I had to leave.

As I tuck Ollie in one last time, I put Mr. William under his arm. I lean down to kiss his small forehead under his messy curls and I can hardly breathe.

I've come to love this little one so much, it's tempting me to stay. But I must go. Before the morning comes. "Good night my love. I'll miss you," I whisper softly.

20

THE LAST TIME

ELLA

The moment Ethan and I find ourselves alone in our bedroom, the air around us changes. I find myself drawn to him, every fiber of my being yearning to feel the comfort his touch provides. He seems to sense my need, drawing me into his arms, pulling me against his solid chest.

We fall onto the bed in a heap of laughter and playful banter. But it soon gives way to a silent understanding, a shared need for closeness. His hands trace paths of fire along my skin. His touch soft yet insistent, stoking the simmering passion between us.

As our bodies move together in a timeless dance, I allow myself to get lost in the intensity of the moment. His touch, his taste, his smell - all intoxicating.

We move together, lost in our own world, one where only we exist. The pleasure that builds within me is tinged with a sharp pang of sorrow. The knowledge of our final night together is an agonizing sweetness to every touch. Every kiss.

As raindrops pitter-patter against the window, I can't help but smile at the sight of him. Ethan is purely breathtaking, his beauty amplified by the soft glow of the lamp beside us.

Every inch of me longs to be with him, to feel his touch. But the thought of not being with him again brings a heavy sadness to my heart.

"Do you feel okay, my love?" he asks, his voice soft and gentle.

I assure him that I am fine, but my heart is heavy. I want to freeze time, to savor every moment with him, to be lost in his arms forever.

As he slowly strips away my clothes, his kisses set my skin ablaze. Every touch, every caress, every breath is pure ecstasy. He goes down on me and teases me with his tongue. I can feel his breath on my pussy and the anticipation is almost too much to bear.

His tongue finally finds my clit, sending waves of pleasure through my body. "I need you," I moan. "I need you now," my desire consuming me.

His face is slick with sweat as he looks up at me, his eyes conveying his own need. I want him inside me, raw and unbridled, with nothing separating us.

Finally, he aligns his cock on my entrance, and I feel him thrust inside, fast and hard. I can't help but moan as his huge cock fills me completely.

Our hands are intertwined, and I wrap my legs around him, lost in the passion of the moment. His face buries in my neck, every thrust making slick sounds that fill the air.

"I love you," I gasp out, feeling the intensity of the moment take hold of me. "I love you so fucking much." I moan as he pounds me. His hand wraps around my neck, and applies a deliciously dangerous amount of pressure to my sides.

I am consumed by desire, my body on fire with need as he fucks me hard, driving me wild with pleasure.

"I love you too." he gasps. He kisses me deeply, his tongue exploring my mouth as he continues to thrust into me. Every movement sends shockwaves of ecstasy through my body. I am drowning in a sensation, lost in the moment with this man who has become my everything.

"Come with me, baby," he moans softly in my ear, his voice heavy with desire. His thrusts are deep and urgent. My body responds to his touch, my skin is on fire with need.

As my orgasm builds, he quickens his pace, driving me harder and higher until I am consumed by pleasure. I can't help but cry out as he fucks me hard. His hand still wrapped around my throat, a sensation of erotic danger envelops me. Every thrust brings me closer to the edge, the anticipation almost too much to bear.

With a final, powerful thrust, I come, my body writhing beneath him as waves of ecstasy wash over me. He follows closely behind, his cock pulsing as he comes inside me, his cum dripping out of my pussy.

I pull him closer, kissing him passionately. My tongue explores his mouth with a hunger that borders on desperation. I want him more than anything, his touch, his taste, his smell. Everything about him is intoxicating. It draws me deeper and deeper into the spinning whirlpool of our ecstasy.

As we lay there, entwined in each other's arms, I know that this is a moment I will never forget. The touch of his skin against mine, the sound of his breathing in my ear, the taste of his lips on mine. Everything about him is perfect.

Even though I know that this will be the last night we share, I can only feel grateful for the time we have spent together. He smiles down at me, his eyes filled with warmth and affection as the tears well up in my eyes. Then spill over onto my cheeks.

Ethan, thinking it's the stress of the past few days, pulls me even closer. He whispers comforting words into my ear, oblivious to the true cause of my tears.

He soothes me, his touch is gentle and loving, until sleep eventually takes over. His breathing grows slow and steady. I listen to the rhythm of his heart, a soothing lullaby that tugs at my heartstrings. I plant one last kiss on his chest, allowing myself a moment of weakness as the tears flow freely.

As I watch him drift to sleep, I etch his peaceful face into my mind, a precious image to take with me. I know that come dawn, I will have to walk away from this man, the man who has given me so much.

And even though my heart breaks at the thought, I know it's something I must do. For him. For Ollie. For us.

21

AN EMPTY SPACE

ETHAN

"Dad, Dad!" The words rumble through my sleep-addled brain, dragging me out of my slumber. Blinking the sleep from my eyes, I focus on the small figure standing beside the bed. Ollie. His hair is an unruly mess, and his big eyes are filled with a childish impatience that brings a sleepy smile to my face.

"What is it, little man?" I ask, my voice still husky with sleep.

"I'm hungry," he declares, as if it's the most urgent matter in the world.

I sit up in bed, stretching out the stiffness from my limbs. "And where is Ella? Isn't she fixing your breakfast?"

Ollie shakes his head, his brows knitting in confusion. "I looked everywhere, daddy. Ella isn't here."

I frown, my heart stuttering in my chest at his words. She wouldn't have left without a word, would she? I shake off the intrusive thought. I reassure myself that she's probably gone out for a morning walk or something.

I hoist Ollie onto the bed, tickling him until he squirms and giggles and his worry forgotten for the moment. "Alright, alright," I laugh, "how about some pancakes for breakfast?"

His eyes light up at the suggestion, "With chocolate chips?"

"Of course, champ. Can't have pancakes without chocolate chips, can we?"

He grins, scrambling off the bed with newfound energy. As I get up to follow him, I can't help but feel an unease creeping in. A lingering worry that I brush aside for the moment, deciding to deal with it later. Right now, I have a breakfast to make and a little boy to keep happy. Ella can wait.

Pancakes made and consumed, Ollie chattering away about his plans for the day. I can't shake the unease that's knotted itself in the pit of my stomach. *Ella, where are you?*

I try her cell, it rings and rings before leading to her voicemail. My brows furrow in concern. This isn't like her.

I check the garage. Maybe she's run to pick up groceries. *Oh no. She's left in her old car. She didn't even take her BMW. That's really strange.*

The morning drags on, with Ollie keeping himself busy with his coloring books. His chatter is a comforting buzz that helps keep the heavy silence at bay. But every tick of the clock, every fleeting minute that passes without a word from Ella is a blow to my composure.

A multitude of scenarios run through my mind, each more distressing than the last. Could she have run off with Matt? Did he threaten her? Has he done something to her? The worst thoughts linger and taunt me. Each question adding to the weight of worry that's crushing my chest.

I stare at my reflection in the mirror, my thoughts ricocheting off the walls of my brain. The man looking back at me is full of fear and uncertainty. This isn't the confident, composed man I'm used to seeing. But then again, life without Ella is a life I'm not used to living.

I try calling her again, my fingers punching in her number with a desperation I can't contain. Again, it rings and rings. Again, it goes to voicemail.

I decide to go to campus for my regular office hours. Maybe I can catch Ella after her Lit class -- if she even attends today,

"Ollie, time to get ready for preschool," I prompt my little buddy.

"Okay Daddy." he replies obediently. "Will Ella pick me up when it's over?"

A wave of heartbreak rushes through me. I've only thought about my own misery. I haven't even considered what this is doing to Ollie.

"No baby, I don't think so. But she'll be home real soon. Okay?" *I hope...what a bluff. How long can I keep him believing she'll be back? Can **I** even keep believing?*

―― *ell* ――

ETHAN

After getting Ollie settled in his classroom, I start to drive toward campus. I begin making a plan to find her. *Where does she usually go after class? Who can I ask?* So many questions I can't answer.

As I arrive on campus, I first head for the library. I know she studies there with her friend Stacey some days. I take the steps two at a time up to the main entrance. I go straight to her favorite table in a quiet alcove.

No one is there. I wander through all the other study areas on the main floor. No Ella. No Stacey.

Dreadful as it may seem, I head toward Sinclair's office. I check the schedule on his door to see where he's lecturing this afternoon. He's on the third floor until 3:00. I bound up the two flights of steps in record time, only to find myself so winded I can't talk.

Once I catch my breath, I burst through the doors of the lecture hall and make a beeline for the podium. Mr. Sinclair stops mid-sentence and glares at me.

"Professor Hartley. To what do we owe this pleasure?" The smirk on his face is so disgusting, I can hardly look at him.

"Can I speak to you for just a moment, Mr. Sinclair? It's quite urgent." I plead with a very serious tone.

"Of course. Continue reading chapter 14. I'll be right back," he instructs his students.

I meet him away from lectern, just out of the view of the class. "Excuse me for interrupting your lecture, Mr. Sinclair. But did Ella Parker attend your class this morning?"

"Why is that so urgent for you to interrupt my lecture?"

"Just answer me damn it! Was she here?"

"No in fact, she was not. Is there a problem?" he inquires with an aloof intonation.

"You could say that. She's my son's nanny and she's missing. I'm trying to find her."

"Oh. Well, you might check with her friend Stacey. They seem to be pretty good friends. But she wasn't in class either."

"Thank you for the information. And again, please accept my apology for the interruption."

As I turn to leave he quips, "If there's anything I can do, let me know. I'm very fond of Ella."

I give him a half-ass salute over my shoulder to acknowledge his offer as I continue out the door. *Yeah, right. I bet you're fond of her, you pervert.*

I have to stay focused on my search for Ella. I'll worry about Sinclair's sleazy ass another time. Now I'm wondering if Ella is even on campus. She's so serious about her classes, it would take something significant to make her skip out on her Lit class.

I'm getting more worried by the minute. One last try. The Steamy Bean. Students study there frequently. Now that she's earning money of her own, it makes sense she would study there instead of the library.

I hear the ding of the door as I enter to the strong aroma of freshly ground coffee. Looking around the crowded café I don't see Ella. But Stacey is sitting alone at a table in the far corner.

I squeeze my way across the standing room only dining room. Stacey sees me as I get nearer to her table.

"Professor Hartley. How are you?"

"It's Ethan. Thanks for asking, Stacey. I'm fine. Well, not really. Have you seen Ella today?"

"Actually no. I was going to ask if she was ill today. I didn't go to Lit class, so I called her to get the assignment. She hasn't answered her phone or texted all day. Did something happen?"

"I'm not sure. She seemed like something was bothering her all day yesterday. Then when Ollie and I got up this morning, Ella wasn't there. I hung around most of the morning, thinking she'd return. But she didn't even take her Beamer. She drove her old junker car. I am at a loss."

"Gee Professor...Ethan. I don't know what to say. It definitely sounds like something's up, but I have no clue. If I think of anything or hear from her, I'll let you know."

"Thanks Stacey. That's nice of you. If you do talk to her, please tell her Ollie really misses her."

"Okay I will. Do you want me to tell her that you miss her too?" she adds with a smirky grin that indicates she's aware of my relationship with Ella.

"Of course," I reply, not knowing what else to say.

22

BACK TO THE PAST

ELLA

The ominous grey building looms in front of me, swallowing the remnants of daylight. My old car's engine rumbles to a stop in the deserted lot. I sit here for a moment, drawing in the musty scent of worn leather seats. The silence interrupted only by my heartbeat throbbing in my ears.

This is it. I'm back to where it all started. I've been living in my car for the whole day now, just like the old times.

Ethan and Stacey have been calling and texting all day. I ought to let them know I'm alright. But then I 'd have to justify why I'm not where I'm supposed to be. My mind is crammed with the things I must face tonight. I don't have enough brain cells to come up with a plausible story. So I don't respond to their messages.

But now, it's time to go. It's time to go to Matt's house. Whether I like it or not.

Clad in jeans and an oversized sweatshirt, I'm stripped of the warmth and safety of Ethan's house. But beneath my plain exterior, there's a resolve. An unyielding determination to right the wrongs.

The air around me tastes bitter and stale, a prelude to the impending storm. I can almost hear the echo of Matt's sinister laugh ringing in the air. He thinks he's won. He believes he holds the strings to my life. How wrong he is.

Tonight, I don't go as a victim. I go as a woman with a plan.

I take one last look at the rearview mirror, my reflection staring back at me. The same features, the same woman who once lived a life caged by Matt's oppression. But the eyes... they are different. They hold a flame, a glint of rebellion.

It's time Matt learns that Ella is not a pawn in his vicious, self-serving game. She's not a woman who bows down to threats and caves to blackmail. She's not the Ella he used to know.

I take a deep breath, letting the cold air fill my lungs, fortifying my resolve. The car door shuts behind me with a deafening thud, marking the end of my past and the beginning of a new chapter. My heart pounds in dread of the scene that will follow.

It's time to face the beast. But this time, the beast doesn't know, he's walking into a trap. I may be alone in this, but I'm far from helpless. And Matt... Matt has no idea what's coming for him.

This isn't about reclaiming my freedom anymore. This is about survival and protecting those I love. It's about fighting back.

As I approach the grim building, I remember Ethan's soft whispers in my ear, his arms around me. The love and warmth I felt in those moments fuel my steps. Those memories I etched in my mind will sustain me in this battle.

I'm not afraid. Not anymore.

Matt wanted to play a game? Well, the game is on. And this time, I intend to win.

The cold metal of the door handle stings my palm as I reach out. I take a moment to collect myself before I tap lightly on the door. The echo of my knock seems to linger in the air, hanging heavily with the weight of the moment.

The door creaks open, revealing Matt, the same smug grin plastered on his face. His arms open in a welcoming gesture. His voice oozes with the sickening sweetness he mastered so well. "Finally, you're back where you belong."

I swallow the bile rising in my throat and force a smile. "Matt," I greet him, letting my voice waver just enough to keep up the pretense of fear. I need him to believe he's in control, for now.

His arm snakes around my waist, pulling me into a hug. The scent of his cologne stings my nostrils and nauseates me. A stark contrast to the comforting warmth of Ethan's fragrance.

I suppress a gag and a shiver, my heart hammers in my chest. This is part of the plan, I remind myself. Don't let him see your repulsion.

Guided by his firm grip, I step into his apartment, each step feeling like a betrayal. But I focus on the task at hand. This is a necessary evil. This is the only way to protect Ethan and Ollie.

The room is exactly as I remember it, a harsh reminder of the life I left behind so long ago. I can do this, I repeat to myself. I am not the same Ella who lived here before. I am stronger. And this time, I have a plan.

Stealthily, I run a finger over the listening device hidden beneath the thick fabric of my shirt. The small bump is almost imperceptible to the touch, but its presence bolsters my resolve. Each word, each action is being secretly recorded.

As I settle into the worn-out couch, my heart pounds in my chest, the steady rhythm reminding me of my mission. The cushion beneath me sinks in places it shouldn't, a tangible sign of a past I am determined not to fall back into.

Matt returns from the kitchen, two cold beers in hand. He extends one to me. Condensation from the chilled bottle dampens my fingertips. I accept it with a weak smile, setting it on the coffee table without taking a sip. My gaze never wavers from him, my senses on high alert.

"I've missed you, Ella," he murmurs, leaning in close. The smell of beer on his breath mingled with the acrid scent of his cologne makes my stomach churn. He moves to plant kisses along my neck, his fingers tightening around my wrist.

Instinctively, I jerk back, my heart hammering in my chest. "I...I need some time, Matt," I stutter, hoping my feigned nervousness is convincing enough.

Matt's expression morphs into one of pure shock as I scramble away from him. The beer bottle on the table tipping and spilling its contents onto the shabby carpet.

"What the fuck, Ella?" His words are ice-cold, a harsh contrast to the heat in his gaze.

"I'm sorry Matt. I'll clean it up." I quickly grab a towel from the kitchen and begin sopping up the spill. "Can we just sit and watch television for a bit? I need to get used to being back here. Please?"

"Yeah. I'm sorry this doesn't compare to the palace you've been living in." His sarcasm flies from his mouth like venom from a snake.

Innocently I reply, "Oh it's not that. I just haven't been around you for a long time and I need to...you know...get used to being with you again."

"Whatever, Ella. Get me another beer while you're in the kitchen," he demands.

Reluctantly I comply, aware that the façade must not reveal my displeasure with serving him. I return with the bottle and take a seat beside him on the couch. Not so close that I'm touching him, but close enough.

He reaches out, putting his arm around my shoulder and tries to pull me next to him. I recoil at the attempt, standing up to excuse myself to the restroom.

Looking at myself in the mirror, I remind myself not to make him too angry too soon. I have to try to get him to say something incriminating that I can use against him. That's my ticket out. I have to get something to hold over his head. If he has more to lose than he gains by hurting Ethan, I may get out of this alive.

I flushed the toilet and splash water on my face to make my escape to the bathroom believable. I double check my wire to be sure it is secure and unseen before returning to the living room with Matt.

"Why don't you tell me what you've been doing in the months since we've been apart? Are you still working at that motorcycle shop over on 5th Avenue?" I don't care one tiny bit, but I need to start a conversation.

"What the fuck, Ella? Get over here by me and let me give you some lovin' from a real man." The implication stings, but I force a slight smile as I slide in next to him.

He starts kissing my neck again. One hand is on my hip, the other draped over the back of the couch. I let him kiss my neck for a second. Then his hand slides up the front of my sweatshirt. My body stiffens in shock. He slides his hand back down, but then under my sweatshirt and up to my breast.

"Matt, I said no. I need time to adjust." I protest and push his shoulders away. As I stand to move away, he grabs my shirt and nearly pulls it off me. I back up farther away from him.

"What did you think Ella? That I wanted you to come here to be my housemaid like at your little palace on the hill? You're here because you're mine." He stalks closer to me as he's talking backing me up against the wall.

His eyes drop to my shirt where the tiny device has slipped free from its hiding place. The tiny red light flickers in the dim light of the room.

His confusion quickly gives way to anger as the realization hits him. "What the hell is this?" He snatches up the listening device with a snarl. The veins on the back of his hand are standing out as he grips the tiny microphone as if to squash it.

I flinch at the raw fury in his voice, but I force myself to hold his gaze, a sudden sense of defiance filling me. The fear, once so prevalent, starts to ebb away, replaced by a sense of resolve.

"It's over, Matt," I say, my voice ringing out in the quiet room. My words hang in the air, the finality of them evident in the stunned silence that follows. I watch as he struggles to process my words. His grip on the device tightening to the point that his knuckles turn white.

He scowls at me for a moment, then suddenly bursts into laughter. The harsh, cruel sound reverberates around the room.

"You think this little toy is going to save you?" He sneers, tossing the device onto the coffee table with a dismissive flick of his wrist. But it misses the table and falls on the floor.

"I'm not the same girl I used to be, Matt," I say, my voice steady despite the pounding of my heart. "You can't control me anymore."

He stares at me, his laughter dying away, replaced by a grim silence. But it doesn't matter. I've said what I needed to say. And, with or without the device, I know I've taken a significant step towards my freedom.

"You need to be taught a lesson," The words barely leave his lips when his hand makes contact with my face. A searing pain blossoms across my cheek, the impact throwing me off balance. I fall onto the cold, hard floor, my body recoiling from the sudden force.

Tears well up in my eyes, blurring my vision, but I force them back. I won't give him the satisfaction of seeing me cry. The metallic taste of blood fills my mouth, and I realize that I've bitten my lip upon impact.

He looms over me, his silhouette blotting out the weak light from the single bulb overhead. The broken pieces of the device glitter maliciously on the floor next to him. With a swift, brutal motion, he grinds his boot into the tiny shards, reducing the precious recorder to nothing more than dust. The sound is final and chilling.

"You're mine, Ella," he growls, his voice a dark echo in the tiny room. "You're only mine."

The words seep into the silence, hanging heavily in the air. The old me would have flinched, would have submitted to his words. But not anymore.

Yes, I cry. I cry for the pain and the fear, but also for the hope and the strength that are slowly emerging from within me. This isn't over. Matt may have won this battle, but I am far from losing the war.

In the terrifying silence that follows his declaration, there's a knock at the door.

23

A Revelation

ETHAN

Back home after I fetched Ollie from school, I realize things are more serious than I thought. No word from Ella. No one has seen or heard from her. There must be something wrong. I won't allow myself to believe she would just walk out on us.

"Daddy, I'm starving. What did Ella make for supper?"

Heart crushing again. We've become so accustomed to Ella taking care of us, it didn't even register I'd have to take on dinner plans myself.

"How about.... PIZZA?"

Ollie smiles and jumps excitedly in circles doing his happy dance for pizza. "Don't forget to get mushrooms on half. That's Ella's favorite."

His words stomp my heart into the ground. How can I destroy my little boy's world again? It was devastating for him when his mother died, but he was so young he didn't really grasp it. But this...This is different. This is very real to him. He's all-in with Ella as his "mommy" person.

After we've finished the pizza we play our guitar songs, trying to keep things as normal as possible. I turn the television on to his favorite PAW Patrol in an attempt to keep Ollie's mind off what is missing...No Ella for him to snuggle with on the couch.

The sun begins its descent, casting long shadows that seem to echo my growing despair. Every tick of the clock is a stinging reminder of the hours Ella has been missing from our lives.

I tuck Ollie into bed, reading him a story, my voice steady despite the storm raging inside me. He drifts off to sleep, his innocent features soothed by the rhythmic rise and fall of his chest. As I plant a soft kiss on his forehead, I can't help but think of Ella. She'd do this with a gentle grace, a calming presence that lulls Ollie to sleep.

Exiting his room, I find myself wandering aimlessly through the house that looms in its eerie silence. My footsteps echo in the quiet, the vacant spaces seeming to mirror the emptiness inside me. Ella's absence has transformed our home into a haunting echo of what it was. A testament to how essential she'd become to our lives.

I sit on the edge of the bed we'd shared, her scent still lingering on the sheets. The memories of our time together, the laughter, the kisses, the whispered promises. They all crash over me like a tidal wave, consuming me in their relentless current.

As the night seeps in, the reality of Ella's absence finally settles. It's deafening, it's overwhelming, it's frightening.

A cocktail of emotion churns in my gut, each one leaving a more bitter taste than the last. Disbelief, confusion, disappointment, anger. But most of all, a crushing sadness that roots me to the spot.

Matt. The name is like acid on my tongue, a sinister shadow that's cast a dark cloud over everything I thought I knew. Could Ella have chosen him? Chosen him over our home, our life, the love I'd only now allowed myself to admit I felt?

The thought is a sucker punch to my chest, robbing me of breath, of reason. We had something beautiful, something I thought was solid. Was it all only an illusion? A mirage that had disappeared as quickly as it had appeared?

How could I have been so blind, so naive to think that she could love someone like me? A man tarnished by his past, juggling too many roles to ever truly succeed in any.

I allow myself to sink into the plush comforter. The sheets are cool, in stark contrast to the warmth she'd infused them with only last night. It all feels so surreal, like a cruel joke, a twisted game.

A gnawing emptiness eats at me, every fiber of my being aching with the loss of her. The world outside continues on its axis, oblivious to my turmoil. Time doesn't stop, even when your world does. It continues, mocking your pain, adding insult to injury.

Sleep evades me, every dream turns into a nightmare where Ella's laughter turns into scorn. I can't give up.

Not yet. Not until I've exhausted every avenue, every possibility. Because Ella is worth fighting for, worth every ounce of pain, every tear shed.

Ella, she's my home, my light, and I won't rest until I bring her back where she belongs - with me.

Happenstance leads me to a crumpled piece of paper under our bed. It's wedged in the corner, a contradiction to Ella's impeccable housekeeping. Curiosity piqued, I retrieve it, smoothing out its scrunched-up form.

The moment my eyes land on the text, my heart constricts in a vice-like grip. The world narrows down to the venomous words scrawled in hasty handwriting.

"Ella," it begins, a familiar name that sends a jolt through me. It's not my hand, not my words. Matt.

"If you don't leave him and come back to me, I'll make sure that everyone knows what's going on between you and your Professor. Come immediately or the entire university will know about your little rendezvous. He'll lose his job, his reputation, everything. Is that what you want?"

The blood drains from my face, replaced by a cold dread that makes my heart stutter in my chest. It is all making sense now.

The sudden departure, her distracted demeanor. This was the trigger.

There is also an address scrawled on the page. He wants her to go there, to meet him, to be with him.

Rage simmers within me, not at Ella, but at Matt, the man who'd dare to use her love for me against her. A feeling of helplessness washes over me. My fingers clenching around the paper, crumpling it once again. But this time, it's not an act of neglect, it's an act of frustration. A helpless anger at the situation, at the unfairness of it all.

I sink down onto the bed, the weight of the truth too heavy to bear. She didn't leave because she wanted to. She left to protect me. Ella, sweet, selfless Ella, had put herself in the line of fire to shield me. The realization calms my aching heart, but it also cuts deep like a sword.

I can't let her sacrifice be in vain. Matt has made this personal, and it's time he learned that no one threatens the woman I love and gets away with it.

The letter might have broken my heart, but it has also lit a fire within me. A fire that won't be extinguished until I have Ella safe in my arms, away from Matt's harmful reach.

Ella is out there somewhere, alone and scared, because of this. This cruel, manipulative threat. I won't let him win. I won't let him take her from me. I will fight for her, for us. This isn't the end. It's only the beginning. Matt started this, but I will finish it.

I grab my phone in desperation.

> Sister, I need your help.
> I need to bring Ollie over
> to spend the night. Please don't
> ask why, just say you'll keep him.

She replies immediately. God bless Alice!

> Of course!
> Whatever you need.
> I'll be watching for
> you.

ETHAN

In a silent neighborhood bathed in the sleepy hues of twilight, I'm waiting in my car. I'm parked a little distance from a nondescript apartment building where Ella may or may not be.

The air inside the car is stifling, oppressive. I could roll down the windows, let in the cooling evening breeze, but I don't. I welcome the discomfort. It's a harsh reminder, like a slap in the face.

It keeps me alert, awake. It doesn't let me drift away into the churning sea of helplessness and regret. Regret that's been threatening to consume me since I woke up to an Ella-less world.

My heart pounds a furious rhythm in my chest. It echoes the ticking seconds that feel like eternities. The address on the threatening letter from Matt is all I have. It's my only lead. The hope that Ella is there, that she's okay, is the only thing keeping me from spiraling into panic.

I check out the area around me to see the low-life neighborhood I'm in. There, in a lot down the block, I see Ella's car. Relief floods over me. At least I know she is here, or least has been.

I dial 911, my fingers trembling as I relay the situation. The woman's voice on the other end of the line is calm and professional. But I can't help the note of urgency that seeps into my words. I tell her everything. From Ella's disappearance to the threatening letter, to the address.

I tell her about Matt, about his assault in my home, about my fears. I implore her to send someone, anyone, as soon as possible.

Once I hang up, all I can do is wait. Wait and hope. It's the hardest thing I've ever had to do. I fight the urge to get out of my car and storm into the apartment building myself. I want to find Ella, to hold her in my arms, to assure her that she's safe, that I won't let Matt hurt her again.

But I can't. Not yet.

So I stay where I am, my grip on the steering wheel white-knuckled, my gaze fixed on the building entrance. My mind runs through a thousand different scenarios, each more horrifying than the last. But I force myself to breathe, to remain calm.

Because if there's one thing I know, it's that Ella needs me to be strong. To have faith. And so, even though every fiber of my being screams at me to do something, anything, I wait.

Time loses its meaning, blurring into an agonizing mixture of fear and anticipation. Then, finally, the wailing siren cuts through the tense silence. A flash of blue and red lights illuminates the street, and my heart leaps in my chest.

The police have arrived.

24

THE END OF THE PAST

ELLA

The knock on the door startles us both, echoing through the room like a shot in the silence. For a moment, neither of us moves, our gazes locked in a battle of wills. My heart is pounding so hard I can hardly hear anything else.

"Open up! Police!" The voice from the other side of the door is stern, authoritative.

A moment of uncertainty passes between us. The blood drains from Matt's face, his dark eyes darting from me to the door and back. His lips curl into a snarl as he takes a threatening step towards me.

"You better stay fucking quiet," he hisses, pointing a warning finger at me. I shrink back, despite my best efforts to stand my ground. He stares at me for a beat longer, his gaze unyielding before he takes a deep breath and turns to face the door.

His footsteps echo ominously in the room as he moves to the door. My heart is a wild drum in my chest, and I'm hyper-aware of the blood that's still trickling down my lip. Every second feels like an eternity, my breath catching in my throat as I watch the scene unfold.

Matt puts on a semblance of a smile, trying to play the part of an innocent man caught in an inconvenient situation. He swings the door open, greeting the policemen with feigned surprise.

"Officers, what brings you here?" His voice is calm, too calm. It sends shivers down my spine.

But the policemen don't smile back. Instead, they stare at him with a steely glare, their eyes darting over his shoulder to the room beyond. I swallow my gasp as one of their glances land on me. There's a flicker of something in his eyes - concern, perhaps? Or is it the glimmer of suspicion?

The room is suddenly heavy with tension, so thick I could cut it with a knife. I can feel the air growing thick around me. My throat is constricting as the gravity of the situation starts to sink in. I'm on the edge of my seat and the room feels like it's closing in on me.

I don't know what's about to happen, but as I sit there staring at the door, one thing is clear. This night is far from over.

The taller of the two policemen steps forward. His stern face emblazoned with determination. "We received a report of a possible abduction. We're here to ensure the safety of the individual involved."

His words are like a sledgehammer to my chest. Matt's eyes flit between the officers, the calm in his face fading. "Abduction?" He laughs nervously. "That's absurd. Ella, tell them."

He turns to me, his face desperate and pleading. But all I can see are his eyes, the same eyes that had looked at me with such contempt and hatred.

I feel the weight of their stares on me, the police officers', Matt's, the world's. But the fear that held me in its grip has eased away, replaced with a new-found resolve.

"Yes," I manage to say, my voice sounding foreign to my own ears. It's meek, shaky, but it's the truth. "Yes, he...he abducted me. He hit me."

The room falls silent at my confession. It feels as if time has come to a standstill, the weight of my words sinking in. Matt's face contorts in disbelief, and then, anger. "You whore!" He spits out, lunging towards me.

But before he can reach me, the officers are on him. The taller one grabs his arms, twisting them behind his back, while the other takes out a pair of handcuffs.

"You are under arrest for the abduction and assault of Ella Parker. You have the right to remain silent. Anything you say can and will be used against you in a court of law…"

His voice fades into the background as I watch Matt, his face reddening in fury, being hauled away. I'm trembling with shock settling in, but there's a strange sense of relief washing over me too. Matt's reign of terror is over. I'm safe.

The ordeal isn't over yet, not by a long shot. There will be questions, statements, court hearings. But for the first time in days, I feel like I can breathe. Like I can finally start rebuilding the shattered pieces of my life. And for now, that's enough.

25

A Bond Stronger Than Fear

ETHAN

As the policemen enter the building, I find myself praying. Praying for Ella's safety. Praying that I haven't failed her, that I'm not too late. Praying that, soon, I'll be able to hold her in my arms again, to tell her how much I love her, how much she means to me.

Because without her, life doesn't seem to make much sense.

The eerie silence of the night is punctuated by the distant city sounds. And the impatient tap of my foot on the car floor. Each second stretches into a minute, each minute into an agonizing hour. The building itself is a silent sentinel. Revealing nothing of the scene unfolding within.

Every fiber of my being is straining towards the entrance of the building. I'm desperate for any sign, any movement, that will tell me Ella is safe. I wipe the sweat off my brow, cursing the lack of information, the helplessness that has me in its grip. The worst enemy is not knowing.

Finally, after an eternity, the front door of the building opens. My heart leaps into my throat as Matt, looking furious and disheveled, is marched out.

He's handcuffed, led by two stern-looking officers. He spits venomous words at them, but they remain unfazed. They steer him towards the waiting police car.

A surge of vindictive satisfaction rushes through me at the sight of him finally paying for his sins. But it's drowned out by a wave of relief so powerful it leaves me lightheaded.

Ella is safe. She's been found. The relief is so overwhelming that I find it hard to breathe. Like I've been underwater for too long and I'm finally coming up for air.

Seeing Matt getting into the police car, I want to step out, to confront him, to unleash my rage. But instead, I sit, watching him. Feeling the tension leaving my body, replaced by profound relief. Ella is safe. That's all that matters.

The sight of her, though, is what finally breaks the dam holding back my emotions. She is escorted out of the building, looking small and vulnerable. Her clothes disheveled and her face pale, but she's unbroken. She's alive. She's safe. And for that, I could kiss the ground she's walking on.

The metallic taste of fear still lingers as I push open the car door. My heart is pounding against my ribcage with an intensity that threatens to shatter it.

The harsh glow of the streetlight paints the scene in vivid detail. Matt's furious eyes, the resolute expressions of the officers. And Ella – her small frame shaking, but an undeniable strength radiating from her.

I take a step forward, and then another. The cool breeze whispers past, carrying the faint sounds of the city. But all I hear is the thunderous rush of blood in my ears. Each stride feels like I'm crossing a monumental chasm. The world narrows down to only her.

As I close the distance, my view of her improves. Her eyes are rimmed red, her lower lip quivers, but she is standing. Holding herself with a bravery that leaves me in awe, she looks up, her eyes finding mine. It feels as if a jolt of electricity passes between us.

"Ella," I breathe out, my voice cracking. I can't hold back any longer. I bolt towards her, my shoes scraping against the concrete in a frenzied rhythm.

She turns toward me as I approach, her eyes widening, a gasp escaping her lips. The moment our bodies collide, it's like coming home after a long, torturous journey. Her body molds into mine, fitting together like two pieces of a puzzle.

I hold her close to me, the softness of her body melting against the hard planes of mine. Her arms wrap around me, clutching at my shirt as if she too needs confirmation that I'm real.

"Ella," I repeat, my voice but a whisper, laden with so much emotion I'm afraid it might break me. I hold her even tighter, burying my face in the crook of her neck, inhaling the sweet scent that's only hers.

She trembles against me, her warm tears soaking the collar of my shirt, but I don't tell her to stop. I let her cry. Let out all the pain and fear. And as her tears fall, my own vision blurs, the pent-up worry and tension of the past hours finally catching up to me.

"Shh...I've got you, Ella" I murmur against her hair, my voice hoarse with emotion. "I've got you, baby girl."

And there, in the cool embrace of the night, under the impassive gaze of the stars, I hold her. I hold her as if my life depends on it. Because in a way, it does. Ella isn't only someone I care for, she's a part of me, a piece of my soul. And I vow to myself, to her, that I won't ever let her face any danger alone again.

Her tears subside, replaced by shaky breaths. I pull back, just enough to see her face. Her eyes, reddened from crying, meet mine. And in them, I see love, relief, and a promise. A promise that we'll face whatever comes together.

The nightmare is over. Ella is safe. And in the comfort of our shared silence, as I hold her close, I promise to keep her safe. Safe in my arms, in our home.

She gets in my car. I'll have someone come for her car tomorrow. Tonight, she's not leaving my side.

The drive home is quiet, an unspoken understanding hanging between us. The empty roads that lie ahead stretch endlessly under the star-kissed night. A mere reflection of the path we had to traverse to reach this point.

As I steer the car through the familiar lanes, I glance at Ella. She's tucked against the passenger side window, thoughts lost in the passing scenery. Her hands are balled into fists in her lap, knuckles white. She's still scared, still shaken, and my heart aches to take it all away.

Once we reach home, we enter through the garage in silence. It's as if we're both afraid to break the fragile peace that the familiar walls offer. I guide her gently towards our room, my arm securely wrapped around her waist, holding her close.

Our home, usually a sanctuary of love and comfort, now feels empty with Ollie at Alice's. But it's also a space for healing, a space for just the two of us, where we can confront and overcome our fears.

We collapse onto the bed, still fully dressed, too drained to care. Ella's body is nestled against mine, her head resting on my chest. I can feel her warm tears soaking my shirt, her shaky breaths against my skin. My hand instinctively rubs her back in an attempt to calm her trembling soul.

"Shh...it's okay, love," I murmur into her hair, my voice no more than a whisper in the quiet room. She clings to me tighter, her fingers grasping at the fabric of my shirt. I can feel her pain, the tremors of her fear echoing through my own body, binding us even closer.

As the night deepens, we lie there, intertwined. The only sounds in the room are our breathing and the occasional sniffle from Ella. I continue massaging her back, my touch gentle yet firm, offering her the comfort she needs.

Time seems to lose its meaning as we remain in each other's arms, the outside world forgotten. Our heartbeats sync in a rhythm as old as time itself, a testament to the bond we share. The air around us pulses with a shared understanding. A silent promise of unwavering support.

Slowly, as the moon casts its soft glow through the window, her sobs subside, her tears dry. But we remain in the same position, clinging to each other. Ella's grip on my shirt relaxes, her body growing heavy against mine. I know she's exhausted, the ordeal of the day taking its toll.

"I've got you, Ella," I assure her again, my voice barely audible. But I know she hears me, feels the promise in my words, as her body relaxes further.

Throughout the night, we remain in each other's arms, holding on as if letting go would mean losing each other. The room is filled with an unspoken love, a silent vow that no matter what, we will face the world together. We drift in and out of sleep, our bodies drawing strength and solace from one another.

As the dawn approaches, breaking through the darkness, it brings a renewed sense of hope. We're still here, still together, stronger and more united than ever. The past may have scarred us, but it's also shaped us, taught us that together we can face anything.

And so, as a new day begins, we continue to hold each other, our bond unbroken, our love steadfast. We may have a long journey ahead, but we know we'll face it together. Because in the end, it's not the destination, but who you're with that truly matters.

26

THE WARMTH OF HOME

ELLA

I open my eyes to the soft morning light seeping through the curtains. Blinking against the sudden brightness, my gaze falls upon the figure lying beside me - Ethan. A sense of relief washes over me, my heart swelling with affection for the man I thought I might never see again.

His strong arms are wrapped securely around me, his breath warm against my neck. He's still asleep, his features softened by the tranquility of sleep. I trace my fingers gently across his stubbled jawline, down his neck, over his broad shoulder. My touch is feather-light, not wanting to disturb his peaceful slumber.

As I lay there, watching him sleep, the magnitude of my feelings for him hits me hard. I love this man more than words can express. He's my anchor, my safe haven in the stormy sea of life. He's given me a love so deep and profound that I can't help but surrender myself to him completely.

The morning sun's rays dance across his face, making him stir in his sleep. His eyes flutter open, and he gives me a sleepy grin. "Good morning, baby," he murmurs, his voice hoarse from sleep.

"Good morning," I whisper. I can't help but smile back, the sight of his tousled hair and sleep-heavy eyes warming my heart. He pulls me closer, his hold on me tightening.

"How did you sleep?" He asks, his eyes searching mine, concern tinging his voice.

"Good... good," I manage to say, looking away from his intense gaze. "How about you?"

He gives a soft chuckle, the sound resonating in his chest. "Like a log," he says, his fingers absently tracing patterns on my arm. "It's been days since I slept this well."

"I'm glad," I whisper, my heart fluttering at his words.

We fall into a comfortable silence, the peace of the morning wrapping around us like a warm blanket. His arms around me feel like home, a place where I am loved, cherished, and protected.

We continue to lie there in the morning light. We share quiet conversations, gentle touches, and sweet kisses. Each word, each touch is an affirmation of our love, a testament to our unyielding bond.

I know that the world outside our little bubble is chaotic. But lying here, with Ethan, I find peace. And as long as we have each other, I know we can face anything that comes our way. Together, we're stronger than any storm.

"Ethan," I begin, my voice shaking slightly. "How... how did you know? About Matt... and where to find me?"

He's silent for a moment, his expression turning thoughtful. His fingers move rhythmically on my back. The gentle movement calms my racing heart.

"I found the letter," he finally says, his voice low. "The one from Matt."

His voice hesitates, his grip around me tightening. "At first, I thought... I thought you had run off with him," he confesses softly.

My heart aches at the pain in his voice. I had caused him so much worry, so much distress.

"I'm so sorry, Ethan," I say, tears welling up in my eyes. "I didn't mean to..."

"Shh, it's okay," he interrupts, pressing a gentle kiss on my forehead. "You were trying to protect me; I know that now. I was just... I was scared I'd lost you."

His words hang in the air, filling the room with a poignant silence. I look up at him. His eyes hold a depth of emotion that makes my breath catch. I see love, relief, fear, and a hint of pain, all swirling in his beautiful green eyes.

"Ethan," I whisper, reaching up to cup his face. "I would never leave you. Not willingly. I love you, Ethan. More than I've ever loved anyone."

His eyes soften at my words, a small smile pulling at the corners of his mouth. "I love you too, Ella. More than I could ever put into words."

With that, he pulls me into a deep, passionate kiss, pouring all his emotions into it. I reciprocate eagerly, losing myself in the warmth and love of his embrace.

The conversation we had was deep, painful even, but it was necessary. It was the beginning of healing, the start of understanding.

"You know, Ella," he says, his voice a near-whisper. "If I ever had to choose between you and my job, I'd choose you without question."

I stare at him, amazed by the strength of his words. The intensity in his eyes makes me breathless, my heart pounding in my chest.

He would give up his job for me? The one thing he had worked for so hard, the one thing he was so passionate about. I blink away the tears prickling at the corners of my eyes, overwhelmed by the enormity of his love for me.

"Ethan," I murmur, cupping his face gently in my hands. "You don't have to..."

"I would," he cuts me off, gently but firmly. "I would, Ella. I would do anything to keep you safe. To keep you with me."

With that, he pulls me closer, his lips claiming mine in another passionate kiss. The taste of him, the feel of him, is familiar and yet so new. It sends shivers down my spine, leaving me wanting for more.

When we finally pull away, my head is spinning, my breath panting. Ethan, ever the observant one, notices my daze and chuckles, the sound low and rich.

"Where's Ollie?" I manage to ask, trying to distract myself from the intensity of the moment.

Ethan grins, running a hand through his hair. "I dropped him off at Alice's. She'll be bringing him back in a while...and she said something about bringing breakfast, too."

He winks at me, and I can't help but laugh. The comfort of the situation, the sheer domesticity of it feels so right. It's a reminder that we're still us, despite everything.

Then, with a mischievous grin, Ethan starts tickling me. I squeal, trying to wiggle out of his grip, but he's too strong. We tumble around the bed, our laughter echoing throughout the room. Filling it with a warmth that feels like home.

The sound of the doorbell chiming through the house stops our playful wrestling. He shoots me a knowing grin before untangling himself from me and hopping off the bed, offering me a hand. We move through the house, hand in hand, a bubble of anticipation building inside me.

As Ethan opens the door, the smile on his face brightens. A small figure barrels past him, running straight into my open arms. "Ella!" Ollie cries out, throwing his tiny arms around my waist as I kneel to his level.

"Hey, buddy," I breathe out, wrapping him in a hug. His little body is warm and full of energy, bringing life to the hushed calm of the morning. But it's exactly what we need.

"Missed you!" He chirps, nuzzling into my neck. His sincerity brings a lump to my throat and I squeeze him a little tighter. "I missed you too, sweetheart."

Behind Ollie, Alice appears, her arms laden with bags of takeout breakfast, a radiant smile on her face. She gives us a casual wave, stepping inside the house as Ethan helps her with the bags. "Morning, lovebirds," she teases, the affection in her voice evident.

Ethan shoots her a mock glare but his eyes are sparkling. "Morning, Alice. Thanks for watching Ollie for us."

Ollie finally releases me, and I rise to my feet, turning to Alice. "Thank you, Alice," I echo Ethan's sentiment, grateful for her support.

She dismisses our thanks with a wave of her hand, though her eyes are soft. "No need for thanks, darlings," She assures, before her gaze sharpens, "Now, let's get this food on the table. I'm starving!"

The morning passes in a warm haze of smiles, hearty food, and heartfelt conversation. It's domestic and comfortable, but most of all, it feels like a family. Our family. Despite everything we've been through, we've come out stronger and closer than ever.

I watch Ollie chatter away, his hazel eyes bright with excitement. Ethan's arm is snug around my waist, and Alice's laughter fills the room. I know this is where I want to be, this is where I belong.

27

BATHED IN LOVE

ETHAN

I'm watching the soft light dance in Ella's hair. As her body cradles Ollie, I'm struck by the gravity of the moment. It's the type of mundane, daily routine that's shared by millions of families across the world. Yet it feels so precious to me, like I'm privy to some profound, secret joy.

Ollie is fighting sleep with all the willpower a three, almost four-year-old can muster. His wide eyes are identical to Ella's in their deep, emerald shade. They're stubbornly blinking as he clings onto consciousness. Ella, patient and tender, coos gently to him. She runs her fingers through his tousled hair.

"Time to sleep, buddy," she murmurs, her voice as sweet as honey.

Ollie scrunches up his face in protest, his tiny fists clenching and unclenching on her shirt. "No," he whines, "I want to build more Legos."

Ella chuckles at his indignant tone, and a ripple of warmth spreads through my chest at the sound. "You can do that in the morning, sweetheart. Okay?"

Ollie grumbles a little, but there's no real fight in him. He looks at her, his eyes growing hazy with sleep, and gives a tired nod. "Okay, mommy."

My heart skips a beat at his words. Mommy. It's such a small word, so innocent and commonplace, and yet it carries a world of meaning. Ollie has never called Ella 'mommy' before, and the weight of it lands heavily in my chest. It grounds me in this beautiful reality.

Ella doesn't correct him. She doesn't freeze or falter. Instead, she smiles, and it's the most radiant smile I've ever seen. Her eyes light up, brimming with unshed tears. There's so much love and warmth in that smile that it takes my breath away.

She leans down, pressing a gentle kiss to Ollie's forehead. Then whispers a quiet, "Goodnight, sweetheart."

Ollie mumbles a sleepy goodnight in return, his small body relaxing against hers. The fight is completely drained from him. Ella lingers for a moment longer. She brushes away the stray locks of hair from his forehead before she finally lays him down on his bed.

Watching Ella, a sense of peace washes over me. We've built a family. A real, loving family. And I wouldn't trade this for the world.

As she turns to me, her eyes still shining, I can't help but pull her into my arms, my heart overflowing with love. "I love you," I whisper into her hair, the words feeling insufficient for the depth of my feelings.

She hugs me tighter, her voice thick with emotion. "I love you too, Ethan."

We stand there for a while, holding each other in the soft glow of the nightlight, our hearts beating in sync. In this quiet moment of tranquility, I know we have a lifetime of mornings, afternoons, and evenings together. A lifetime of loving and being loved.

And that's more than enough for me.

We wander into the living room and Ella slips into the kitchen.

The clink of glasses being set on the table brings me back from my reverie. Ella's returned from the kitchen, carrying two glasses of red wine. Her smile is soft in the dim light of our living room. She hands me a glass and I accept it gratefully, noticing the curves of her petite frame.

"You know," I begin, swirling the wine in my glass, the rich aroma rising up to me. "You should really stop wearing only a shirt when we're at home."

Her eyebrows shoot up in playful surprise. She throws her head back, laughter echoing throughout the room. "How do you know I'm only wearing a shirt?" She teases, her eyes dancing with amusement.

My heart beats faster at her challenge, a thrill shooting down my spine. Not one to back down, I place my glass on the coffee table and reach out, pulling her by the waist towards me. She gasps, the surprise evident in her eyes, but she doesn't resist as I lift her and settle her onto my lap. I can feel the heat of her skin through the thin fabric of the shirt. The contours of her body are pressed against mine, sending my heart into overdrive.

"Ethan!" She squeals, her arms instinctively winding around my neck for support. But her protest is half-hearted, her grin betraying her enjoyment.

I chuckle, the sound rumbling in my chest. "Just proving my point," I say, wrapping my arms around her waist.

And I was right, she wasn't wearing anything else but one of my shirts.

Her nipples harden against my palms, a primal urge takes over me. I can't help but let out a low growl. The taste of her skin, the scent of her hair, the sensation of her body pressed against mine - it all drives me wild with lust.

My hands move over her curves, mapping them out with a hunger that borders on desperation. She shivers and moans in my ear, her breath hot against my skin. And I know that I want her like I've never wanted anything before.

My cock grows harder by the second, straining against the fabric of my pants. I can barely contain myself, the need to take her overwhelming every other thought in my mind. And as I look into her eyes, I know that she feels the same way.

I pull her closer, our bodies melding together with a fierce hunger that sends a shiver down my spine. I know that this time, I will fuck her until we're both completely spent.

A wicked glint sparkles in her eyes as she pushes herself off my lap. She breaks the connection but not the intimate bubble we're in. "I'm going to take a bath," she declares, her voice light and playful. "Wanna join me?"

My breath stops at the invitation laced with a promise of shared warmth and closeness. There's a cheeky grin on her face, her eyes full of mischief and allure. I find myself answering even before I've processed her question. "Yeah," I reply, my voice deeper, huskier.

She extends her hand to me and I take it, letting her lead the way. We wind through the quiet house, a thrill of anticipation coursing through me. I can't help but admire the way she moves, the grace in her steps, the confident sway of her hips.

Reaching the bathroom, Ella flips on the lights. The room is instantly awash in soft, ambient lighting. She turns the water on and within seconds, steam begins to fill the room, making the air warm and moist.

I watch as she pulls her shirts off and drops it to the floor. I follow suit. I can't tear my eyes away from her, the sight of her vulnerability and beauty igniting a fire within me.

Finally, she steps into the tub, the water lapping against her skin. I join her, our bodies submerging into the warmth. The warmth of the water envelops us. The heat seeps into our skin, dissolving any lingering tension.

She straddles me, grinding her hips against mine, and I can feel myself getting harder and harder.

I let her take control, and she rides me hard and fast, her moans growing louder and louder with each thrust. I can't help but spank her ass, the sound echoing throughout the bathroom. And driving her wild with pleasure.

But soon, I can't take it anymore. I grab her roughly and press her against the bathtub, her back arching in pleasure. Her pussy is aching for more, and I tease her mercilessly. I brush her clit teasing her entrance with my cock.

She loses herself in the sensation. Her moans grow louder and more desperate with each passing moment. I know she's close, so I keep rubbing and teasing until she's begging for more.

"What the hell, Ethan?" she demands. "Fuck me already!"

Finally, I can't resist any longer. With a fierce hunger, I push myself inside her, and she moans in ecstasy. As soon as I am all the way inside her, she comes, her whole body trembling and her legs shaking.

But I don't stop. I fuck her even harder and faster. Ella's eyes roll back in her head as I pound into her, my cock slamming against her cervix with each thrust. I can feel her walls tightening around me.

Her moans grow more and more desperate with each passing moment. I'm lost in a haze of lust, my body moving on autopilot as I seek to satisfy the primal urges that have taken hold of me.

"Fuck, Ethan," she gasps, her fingers digging into my back. "Harder, please."

I oblige, pulling out almost all the way before slamming back into her. The force sends her bouncing up and down on my lap. She cries out, her breasts jiggling with the force of my movements.

She arches her back, her pussy squeezing me tighter, and I know that she's close for a second one. But I don't want to let her come yet. I pull out completely, leaving her panting and frustrated. She glares at me, her eyes flashing with a mix of anger and lust.

I grin. I love teasing her. But I'm not done yet. I get inside her again, and thrust real hard. I keep fucking her, my movements becoming more and more frenzied as my own climax builds deep within me. I can feel her pussy clenching, her walls squeezing me hard and I know that I'm getting close.

With one final, powerful thrust, I come, my cock pulsing inside her as I shoot my hot cum deep into her pussy. She cries out, her body convulsing with pleasure. I hold her tight, feeling her body shake against mine as we both come down from the high.

"That was amazing," she says, her voice a whisper.

I grin, feeling a sense of satisfaction wash over me. "Glad you enjoyed it," I say, holding her close.

Once our shared moment of passion subsides, we lounge in the warm water. Our bodies are entwined and content. Ella's nestled against me, her head resting on my shoulder.

I caress her gently, running my fingers along the curves and dips of her body, tracing paths on her damp skin. The tenderness of the moment seeps into my bones, turning my heart heavier with love for her.

"I love you, Ella," I murmur into her hair, my voice echoing in the steam-filled bathroom. She turns in my arms to face me, her eyes shining with a love that matches mine.

"I love you too, Ethan," she responds in a whispered voice. Her fingers reach up to trace the lines of my face, and I lean into her touch, closing my eyes at the softness of her hands. There's a promise in her words, a vow of forever that we're both ready to keep.

After we finish our bath, I help her out of the tub, wrapping a fluffy towel around her. We move out into our bedroom, where I help her dress in one of my oversized T-shirts that she loves so much. I slip into a pair of boxers, and we collapse onto the bed, exhausted but blissfully happy.

As we lay there, basking in the afterglow of our love, I pull her closer. I relish the feel of her curled against my side, her breathing slowly syncing with mine. This is our reality now. No more threats, no more running away. Only us, living our life, a picture of domestic bliss.

Morning finds us in the same position, her curled into me. Her hair is sprawled over the pillow, rays of sunshine dancing over her face. I watch as Ollie trots into the room, a wide grin on his face as he sees us. "Daddy, Mommy," he chirps, and my heart swells at the sight.

This is my life now, a life filled with love, peace, and happiness. A life where I wake up next to the woman I love, our son in the next room. A life where we are a family. And I wouldn't trade it for anything in the world.

This is our happily ever after. Our quiet, perfect, beautiful happily ever after.

28

Epilogue

ELLA

My eyes open to the familiar light seeping through the curtains. I smile before realizing something unfamiliar—Ethan is not beside me. Sitting up, I listen and look around the room before remembering—today is the day.

I relax back into the pillows, and I close my eyes. Ethan and Oliver left early to spend the morning with Alice. Ethan adheres to the crazy superstition that we should not see each other until the wedding. I'll have to wait until noon when the ceremony begins to see the love of my life.

I slip on a pair of my comfy jeans and one of Ethan's over-sized shirts. On my way to the kitchen, I'm interrupted by Stacey ringing the bell and pounding on the door.

When I let her in, she holds a bag from Gas-n-Go. "Blueberry muffin for the bride," she announces, and we laugh and hug. "Like old times," she adds.

"Not exactly. I'm not sneaking into the Y and I'm not starving," I chuckle.

I help Stacey inside with her industrial size make up kit, her dress bag and purse. As I pass the window, I notice a white panel van pulling into the drive.

A young man, with boyish blonde hair and a muscular build approaches. When I go out to meet him, he introduces himself as Gerard. "Professor Hartley told me exactly how to set up, but if there is anything you want to change, let me know. Just point me in the right direction, and I'll get started."

I walk with Gerard to the stairs leading to the terrace where Ethan and I decided to have the ceremony. Stacey is close on my heels, her eyes bright with curiosity.

"And this is Stacey, my maid of honor," I say as Gerard surveys his workspace.

"Very pleased to meet you," she says, extending her hand. "I'll be happy to help with anything you need."

I smile at Stacey's interest in the student wedding planner, and then I excuse myself to go inside.

I sip coffee and watch from the kitchen window. Stacey and Gerard turn the terrace into a picture-perfect setting. Our theme is simple. White pillars topped with vases of yellow roses. Sprigs of fresh lavender complement the scene.

Gerard then assembles a simple brass archway. White wispy panels floating on either side. He and Stacey exchange goodbyes as he pulls away and Stacey heads inside.

"He is divine, Ella. And he's coming back in a bit with the music students. Now let's make you the most beautiful bride in the history of the world."

We make our way to the guest suite where Stacey gets to work, single-handedly doing my makeup and hair.

When it's time, she helps me into my gown. The cutout white lace of the sweetheart neckline lays against my tanned skin and bare shoulders. The lace follows closely along my silhouette before sweeping into a mermaid train.

I opted for no veil. My hair is swept back and intertwined with baby's breath near the crown, then cascading down my neck and back.

Stacey arranged for a large showroom mirror from the bridal shop to be delivered and set up in the room. Seeing my reflection for the first time, I realize how talented Stacey is.

I tell her, "You should have a side gig doing beauty prep for brides on their wedding day. Your catch phrase can be 'I'll make you the most beautiful bride in the history of the world.'"

Stacey laughs at the thought of it. "I can't make just anyone a beautiful bride. You were beautiful before I started. I just touched you up a bit."

I smile at her compliment, but still...as I look back to the mirror, I can't help but remember my life before Ethan. It's hard to believe the bride I'm looking at now ever lived in a car.

I'm so blessed to have landed here with the man of my dreams and his sweet son. It's more than I could ever have hoped for.

ETHAN

"Yes, Ollie, you can see Ella as soon as I park the car," I explain. "But Daddy can't see her right now. We'll all be together on the terrace very soon. You just stay with Ella, okay?"

Ollie is already out of the car, running toward the house. As I walk around to the back, the terrace is even more striking than I imagined. I tried to think of everything when I was planning it with my student, Gerard. Ella will be pleased...I hope.

"Any jitters, brother?" Alice interrupts my thoughts.

"Not one. Today is the day. I've never been more certain of anything." I reply. "I just want everything to be perfect for Ella. She deserves this and so much more."

I continue to the terrace as a smiling Alice catches up with Ollie. She takes him inside to meet up with Ella. He looks so grownup dressed in his grey tux, Ella will be so proud.

ELLA

Soft strains of instrumental music flow through the open window as I peek through the curtains hoping for a glimpse of Ethan. *He has arranged every detail to make this day the best day of my life.*

I scan the scene, where Alice is conferring with a man in a chef coat. I see them under the small white tent where the luncheon will be served. From the looks of their close conversation, I suspect he is more than a friend to Alice.

And then I see Ethan. He looks so handsome in his gray tuxedo. He's standing near his four students providing the music. The musicians are seated on the terrace in white chairs. The skip of my heartbeat and the catch in my throat assure me of my love for this man and the life he is providing me.

"Ella, can we go now? Stacey says it's time," Ollie has quietly joined me, and I take his hand in mine, with a last look in the mirror.

"Come on already, the musicians are on their last number before our entrance. It's time to start this show," Stacey says impatiently. "You are radiant,' she adds.

I follow Stacey through the hallway of the guest suite. I watch as she steps through the doorway to descend to the terrace.

"Alright, Ollie, it's our turn. Today is the day. I love you, champ."

"I love you too, Mommy," Ollie replies.

I squeeze Ollie's hand and grasp my orchid bouquet as I step into the shining warmth of the noon sun and a new life.

THE END

Thank you for reading ***Billionaire's Nanny: Destiny Soul Mates.***

If you loved this book, you'll love ***A Baby with my Billionaire Surfer.***

Sure I kissed her, but that was playing a game at a party with 100 of our closest friends.

When I innocently offered to coach Violet for the upcoming surf competition, I never thought it would go this far.

As the storm blew in off the ocean, our only option was to run to the empty lifeguard tower.

So now I'm stuck with my best friend's little sister...But she's not so little anymore.

Outside the tower, cold winds are roaring. Inside the sizzling seduction is electrifying.

Violet's parents have arranged for her to marry a guy she barely knows and doesn't even like. They tell her she has no choice.

Now that she's carrying my baby, I don't think I can let her go through with it.

I will do whatever it takes to stop the wedding, no matter the consequences.

Scan to get *A Baby with my Billionaire Surfer.*

Check out this excerpt...

VIOLET

As I watch my reflection in the mirror, my mind drifts to yesterday afternoon on the beach. Ryan Ryder, the notorious heartthrob. Me pinned beneath his chiseled body, a sea of shock and amusement dancing in his eyes.

His tanned, toned body against mine, the heat radiating from his skin, and the soft sand beneath us. I blush even thinking about it, and the giddy smile refuses to leave my face.

Heat floods my cheeks as I imagine his lips trailing down my neck, his hands sliding down to...

"Violet!" Alec's voice disrupts my thoughts, pulling me out of my imagination. I immediately jerk back to reality.

I blush harder, thankful that Alec can't see my face right now. "Y-Yeah?"

"Are you ready yet? You've been in there for an eternity," Alec calls from down the hall.

"Ryan's party isn't until tonight, you know!"

I roll my eyes, fighting back a smile. Oh, if only Alec knew. The last thing I need is my brother teasing me about my daydreams.

Especially when they involve a certain hunky lifeguard...

I text my best friend Alissa about the encounter with Ryan at the beach yesterday.

***If you tell anyone that I daydream about Ryan,
I swear I will wring your neck.
Especially Alec. I mean it too!***

Who me?
I'd never tell anyone what a crush you have
on the lifeguard known as Ryan.
My lips are sealed.

Yeah, right. Like I'd believe that for a second. But she's my best friend and I trust her not to humiliate me in front of a crowd.

Still giggly from my Ryan daydream, I hop in the shower. We leave in an hour.

I choose a blue dress that hugs my every curve. Simple but making a statement. It's the perfect camouflage for a beach party.

Especially since we've told our folks we're off to a movie with friends. Friends who need to drop off a document at the Ryders on the way home. Our backup story if we get busted for partying at Ryan's.

Alec is anxious again. "Time's up Vi. We'll be late for the movie." His voice emphasizes 'movie' in case parents are listening.

"Coming!" I call back at Alec.

Giving my long, wavy ginger hair a last-minute fluff, I take in my reflection. My favorite silver pendant, a gift from Mom, lays against my chest, a tiny beacon of courage.

I breathe deeply, reminding myself I'm not that little girl anymore. I'm almost thirty...well I will be in two or three years...or four. I make my own decisions, even if it means bending the truth a little for a night of fun....

...As we step onto the party deck, loud music and chattering voices fill the air. A few brave, or maybe just drunk, souls are stripping down for a dip in the luxurious heated pool. Some are socializing in the massive sunken hot tub. If socializing means groping each other, then yeah, they're socializing.

My eyes drift across the crowd, seeking one particular face. Then I spot him. Ryan. Tall, muscular, with that beach blonde hair that always looks effortlessly styled. He's in the kitchen, drink in hand, and there's someone with him. It takes a moment for the realization to hit me.

Gemma. His ex.

Look at these 5-star reviews...

...It was a page turner and the suspense was intense. I was at the edge of my seat and I couldn't put it down...

A great read that has everything one could hope for, billionaire, best friend's little sister, surprise pregnancy. And the chemistry between Ryan and Violet was super hot...

...The characters were amazing, and I loved how their love grew. I felt everything the author wrote and wanted me to feel...

...Some drama and steam as Ryan is determined to claim her as his...

This is a stand-alone, billionaire, brother's best friend, arranged marriage, surprise pregnancy romance. There are explicitly steamy scenes and little adult language, but no violence, rape, incest, or menage. ***And a Happily-Ever-After ending, of course!***

Scan to get A Baby with my Billionaire Surfer NOW!!

Printed in Great Britain
by Amazon